# MURDER AT THE BOXING CLUB

A 1920S COZY HISTORICAL MYSTERY

A GINGER GOLD MYSTERY
BOOK TWENTY

LEE STRAUSS

*Murder at the Boxing Club*

Copyright © 2022 by Lee Strauss

Cover by Steven Novak, Illustrations by Tasia Strauss. All rights reserved. No part of this book may be reproduced in any form or by any electronic or mechanical means, including information storage and retrieval systems, without written permission from the author, except for the use of brief quotations in a book review.

Library and Archives Canada Cataloguing in Publication

Title: Murder at the Boxing Club / Lee Strauss.

Names: Strauss, Lee (Novelist), author.

Series: Strauss, Lee (Novelist). Ginger Gold mystery ; 20.Description: Series statement: A Ginger Gold mystery ; book 20 Identifiers: Canadiana (print) 20220228485 | Canadiana (ebook) 20220228493 | ISBN 9781774092217 (hardcover) | ISBN 9781774092194 (softcover) | ISBN 9781774092200 (IngramSpark softcover) | ISBN 9781774092224 (Kindle) | ISBN 9781774092231 (EPUB) | ISBN: 978-1-77409-339-9 (bookvault) | ISBN: 978-1-77409-408-2 (D2D)

Classification: LCC PS8637.T739 M8723 2022 | DDC C813/.6—dc23

# GINGER GOLD MYSTERIES

## (IN ORDER)

Murder on the SS *Rosa*
Murder at Hartigan House
Murder at Bray Manor
Murder at Feathers & Flair
Murder at the Mortuary
Murder at Kensington Gardens
Murder at St. George's Church
The Wedding of Ginger & Basil
Murder Aboard the Flying Scotsman
Murder at the Boat Club
Murder on Eaton Square
Murder by Plum Pudding
Murder on Fleet Street
Murder at Brighton Beach
Murder in Hyde Park
Murder at the Royal Albert Hall
Murder in Belgravia

Murder on Mallowan Court
Murder at the Savoy
Murder at the Circus
Murder at the Boxing Club
Murder in France
Murder at Yuletide
Murder at Madame Tussauds
Murder at St. Paul's Cathedral

# 1

Ginger Reed, also known by some as Lady Gold, held up two clip-on earrings to her ears, one a hoop of small turquoise beads and the other a delicate crystal-encrusted teardrop. The beauty of the current short and sassy hairstyles was that they allowed for ear decorations to be easily seen, and Ginger's red bob was evidence of that. She chose the teardrops, then completed her make-up: smoky shadow reaching her thinly plucked, arched eyebrows; a circle of red parked on each cheekbone; and her lips shining with luxurious pink.

Catching her husband's warm hazel eyes through the mirror's reflection, she asked, "What does one wear to a boxing match?" She answered her own question, saying, "Subdued is preferred, I gather."

"Sports betting attracts commoners, high society,

and highbrow alike," Basil said. "You'll stand out more no matter what you choose, I'm afraid."

Ginger selected a burgundy suit with a pleated skirt that fell to mid-calf, a button-down jacket with a matching belt that rested low on the hips, and a matching cloche hat. If it weren't for Marvin Elliot being in the ring, she wouldn't be going. She despised these boorish events and thought them rather reminiscent of the barbarism of the Roman circus.

"You're sure Marvin will be all right?" Ginger asked as she donned a blouse.

"He's been fighting since he joined the navy," Basil said. "He's young, energetic, and has strong survival instincts."

Ginger groaned. "He needn't require survival instincts if he'd behaved."

Marvin was the cousin of Scout, Ginger and Basil's adopted son, and had recently been dishonourably discharged from the navy.

Basil glanced over, pausing at his wardrobe where he was selecting his attire. "You don't have to come, love, if you find it so very disagreeable."

Ginger glanced about the room, once her childhood chambers, which had been redecorated to suit her maturity and marital status. The heavy, ornately carved wood furnishings included a sitting area with a small table and two gold-and-white striped chairs in front of the windows. The thought of spending the evening lounging in the comfort of her four-poster bed, playing with her nine-month-old daughter Rosa, and then later reading Mrs. Christie's *The Big Four* did seem appealing.

However, other wives and sweethearts attended these events, and if Basil continued attending, she wanted to know what the fuss was about. Seeing Marvin again would be a bonus, as she hadn't seen the young man for a few months after his employment with the circus. Ginger had been relieved when he'd chosen to stay behind after the circus moved on, but she did wish he'd found a less dangerous way to earn a living.

"You're sure Marvin is up to the task?" Ginger asked. She slipped on the suit jacket, then fastened the buttons and the belt. "It seems like this has all happened so fast."

"The lad has had a most extraordinary rise in the rankings," Basil conceded. "A testament to his talent."

"But isn't he fighting that Sid Lester fellow? A professional?"

Basil raised a brow. His brown hair, shaved short on the sides, shone with grey, and the top was oiled and neatly combed over to one side. A decade Ginger's senior and now in his forties, Basil remained attractive even with deepening wrinkles and greying temples.

"You've heard about Sid Lester?" he said.

Ginger nodded. "I've been following the fights in the newspapers. He looks like a big man and is much older than Marvin."

"The photographs are misleading," Basil said. "They're both middleweight. Lester's face has taken more of a beating." He put on a short summer jacket instead of his usual trench coat, then selected a flat cap, a marked change from his usual trilby. He must've noticed Ginger's questioning look as he explained, "I don't want to look like a copper. It makes folks uneasy."

The flat cap made Ginger *uneasy*, as it wasn't a look she was used to seeing on Basil. "Are we ready?" she asked.

Basil held out his hand. "Let's go."

Ginger loved how they still felt like newlyweds, married only three years after all. They stopped at the nursery to give Rosa a kiss and a hug. Their daughter had pulled herself to a standing position in her crib, holding on to the metal rails with fat little fingers. She bounced excitedly when she spotted her parents, and Ginger's heart filled as Basil swooped his little daughter into his arms—surprising Abby Green, the nanny—and patted Rosa's dark hair. Except for her green eyes, which she'd got from Ginger, she looked like her daddy.

After taking her turn to hold Rosa, Ginger handed the child back to the nanny. "Good night, Rosa."

Leaving the nursery, Ginger and Basil headed down the long corridor to the broad, curving staircase that opened to the entranceway. A large chandelier hung from the high ceiling and sparkled over the polished marble floors. They were halfway down when thirteen-year-old Scout raced around the corner and up the stairs. Boss, Ginger's little Boston terrier, was on his heels.

"Whoa!" Basil said. "Where's the fire?"

His cheeks flushed and straw-coloured hair a mess, Scout huffed, "Are you going to Marvin's fight?"

"We are," Ginger said.

Scout's round eyes blinked rapidly. "Can I come? Please! I want to see Marvin fight!"

Ginger shot Basil a sideways glance. She'd hoped they would've been able to leave before Scout returned from his riding lesson.

"Not this time," Ginger said. "We're about to depart, and we'll be late."

"I'm ready!" Scout insisted.

"Son," Basil said, "you smell like a horse. And you're too young to get in."

Ginger wasn't sure if this was true, though she hoped there would be an age limit to entry. Regardless, she was ready to impose one on her son.

Scout's shoulders, thin yet widening with pubescence, drooped. "I hate being so young!"

"Enjoy your youth whilst you can," Ginger said. "Now, go upstairs and bathe before the whole house smells like a stable."

Scout trudged upstairs in reluctant defeat. Even so, he'd become much more amiable since the debacle at the circus. Ginger had to acknowledge that their son, having spent ten years struggling on the streets of

London, would never fully conform to the new world of which he was now part. His disastrous experience at Kingswell Academy had proven that he'd never fit in with the children of the elite.

In the back garden, Basil reversed his forest-green 1922 Austin out of the garage, then jumped out to open the passenger door for Ginger. Once they were both seated inside, Basil turned to her and said, "If it gets too distasteful for you, just say the word, and we'll leave."

Ginger patted Basil's arm with appreciation. "I'll do my best to stomach it."

"I'LL WAGER you've never been to a venue quite like this before," Basil said as he and Ginger headed to the second-tier section of the Bethnal Green Boxing Club in the East End. Their hard wooden seats sat on a balcony that surrounded a boxing ring one floor below, surrounded by collapsible seats arranged in rows almost right up to the side of the ring.

"No, I certainly haven't," Ginger said, checking their ticket stubs.

"Yes, this is the right spot, my dear. I didn't think you wanted to be in the lower stall section. I think it might be rather close to the kind of action planned for tonight." He pointed down at the scene below them. "It's not exactly the Royal Ballet or the London Symphony Orchestra."

"Quite." Ginger scanned the lower-floor seats.

Basil felt concerned that his wife would want to leave after the first round. He hoped that by sitting higher up and away from the ring, there at least would be little danger of spittle or sweat from the boxers hitting them. That, he thought ruefully, would guarantee a quick exit.

"That's where the judges and the press gallery sit." Basil pointed to some empty seats beside the ring. A long wooden table with a large golden boxing bell was placed in the middle.

"The ring official just hits the bell with his palm at the beginning and end of every round," Basil remarked.

"No doubt a lot of training is required for that job," Ginger said sarcastically.

"Well, at least one would have to keep one's eye on the clock."

"I might be doing the same," Ginger said under her breath.

"I heard that." Basil smiled and nudged her with his shoulder. "I hate to inform you, but these fights have the potential to go a full ten rounds."

"What fun."

Basil chuckled. "I'll bet you your next fancy hat you'll be surprised at how the time goes."

"I don't doubt that," Ginger said, "but for your information, my hats aren't fancy. They're elegant and fashionable. You don't spot a Reboux original from Paris and call it fancy."

"Well, no, I wouldn't, of course," Basil said with a hint of tease in his voice. "No . . . the boys down at the Yard would call it fancy, but not me." He adjusted his flat cap. "Inspector Sanders, for example, is a good man but certainly not in tune with the latest fashions like I am."

That earned him a raised eyebrow and a wry smile from Ginger.

Quiet for a moment, Basil then said, "The Bethnal Green Boxing Club Hall has been in existence since 1884." Thinking that perhaps a little history would make Ginger more comfortable with her surroundings, he went on. "It seats about two hundred people at its fullest, which I think we might see tonight."

He waved his arm expansively around the large room. The crowd in the packed hall comprised mostly of men, had a surprising number of women as well. He held up a printed brochure. "This club has produced a lot of champion boxers, including Sid Lester."

"May I?" Ginger reached for the brochure.

"He's a formidable pugilist, all right." Basil nodded at an image of a shirtless, barrel-chested man with his bare fists held up in front of him. Sid Lester's nose was unnaturally crooked, and his eyes looked like dark, soulless pools as he glared at the camera. "They nicknamed him 'The Midnight Train' because he comes up with the goods every night right on time," Basil said. "Even the press is afraid to interview him. They say he's like an enraged bull in the ring." Basil blew air out of his cheeks. "He's been London's champion middleweight boxer for almost eight years running now. His hands are larger than what would seem suitable for his size, and his punches seem to go right through his opponents. In fact, his gloves are custom-made to make room for his big fists. They are like steam shovels."

Ginger's hand went to her throat. "And this is the fellow Marvin is fighting tonight?" She stabbed the photograph of Marvin with a long fingernail. "He looks..."

Basil placed a reassuring palm on Ginger's arm. "From what I've been told," he started, "Marvin is exceptionally fast in the ring."

"He will have to be!" Ginger stared at the two men in the brochure with a deep concern written all over her face.

"I'll tell you one thing," Basil continued. "He must be very talented to have risen in the ranks this fast to get a shot at Sid Lester. Perhaps in part due to how outspoken Marvin has been with the press. After winning his last few fights, he seems to have taken on the role of showman just as much as that of a boxer, perhaps learning from his circus days. Some of the newspapers have started calling him 'Marvin the Mouth'. He appears to enjoy goading his opponents."

Ginger stared at Basil incredulously. "Marvin the Mouth?"

Basil hurried to defend the moniker. "Last week,

during an interview with the *London Sports Gazette*, he called Lester a gorilla, saying he was as ugly as an old barn."

Sniffing, Ginger said, "That seems unwise."

"Well, if he defeats Lester, he'll win the title of London Middleweight Champion, which carries a lot of prestige and a generous purse. Quite a feat for a young man by just 'throwing leather about', as they say in the boxing vernacular."

Ginger adjusted her hat. "You mean pawing at each other and jostling about in the ring."

"You could put it that way," Basil said with a chuckle. "But if he wins here, he might even go on to fight Britain's champion at the Royal Albert Hall or something."

"I just hope he survives," Ginger said. "Perhaps a good brain rattling is what he needs to come to his senses."

"I think the fight is about to start." Basil pointed at a middle-aged man wearing a dinner jacket who entered the ring carrying a megaphone.

"*Ladieees* and gentlemen," the ring announcer shouted, and the crowd grew instantly quiet. "On behalf of the London Boxing Commission and the East End of London Sports League, I welcome you to this fine facility tonight. We have an exciting bout for you all, and I hope you are ready for it. Let's get right to it, shall we? In the challenger's corner, weighing ten stone nine, a young man who has already made quite a name for himself in the world of both bare-knuckle and Queensberry Rules, from Cheapside, the Marvellous *Maaaarviiiin* Elliot!"

The applause was muted. There were even a few boos in the crowd.

"It seems that his antics in the press haven't helped him," Ginger said.

The sinewy form of Marvin Elliot entered the ring accompanied by a black man carrying a small wooden stool and a leather kit. Marvin was shirtless but wore white shorts, black leather boots, and red boxing gloves. Jeering at the crowd, he bounced in his corner while banging his gloves together.

"He looks good," Basil remarked. "Trim, fit, alert."

"Colourful," Ginger added. "What is meant by Queensberry Rules?"

"It refers to a set of generally accepted rules. For example, the boxers must wear gloves, there's one minute between rounds, no wrestling . . . things like that. Regulations that make the sport a little less barbaric."

"I could add to that code," Ginger offered.

Marvin's gaze moved to their area in the auditorium, and Ginger waved, but he didn't seem to notice.

"You shouldn't wave at him like you're his mother or something," Basil scolded mildly.

"Why on earth not?"

"Well, it might put him off to know you're here. The same goes for me. It's best he stays focused."

"Nonsense," Ginger said. "I should think it would make him feel like someone in this crowd is rooting for him."

"But you're not really. I suspect you'd like to see him lose the match if you had your way. Not injured badly but discouraged enough to stop pursuing this line of work. Am I right?"

Ginger lifted a thin shoulder non-committally. "And what about you?"

Basil opened his mouth to disagree, but as Marvin's opponent emerged, with hard muscles, a heavy brow, and a crooked nose, Basil decided that perhaps Ginger had a point.

"And in the champion's corner, ladies and gentlemen," the announcer shouted with great exuberance as cheers rose from the crowd. "From right here in London's East End, the 'Locomotive', 'the Midnight Train', the man with dynamite in his fists and thunder in his arms, weighing eleven and a half stone, the one, the only *Siiiiiid Lesterrrrr!*"

The crowd erupted with such a roar it caused Ginger to put her hands over her ears.

Basil grimaced. It'd been a mistake to bring his wife. This crowd wasn't on Marvin's side. He feared carnage.

## 2

*G*inger could barely conceal her shock and dismay as Sid Lester strutted towards the ring, hoisting his muscular body between the ropes stretched open by his team members. He was wearing black shorts and black leather laced boots. The ceiling lights reflected off oiled shoulders. Raising one gloved hand in the air, he encouraged the crowd to cheer wildly again. An eager, breathless mob, they hungered for blood.

It turned Ginger's stomach, and her newly roused maternal instincts wanted to march down to the ring, grab Marvin by his arm, and rescue him from certain harm. Instead, she took Basil's hand and squeezed it.

The referee, a serious-looking man in his mid-fifties, motioned the two fighters to the ring's centre. Marvin, lighter in weight and shorter in stature, had to crane his neck to meet his opponent's malevolent gaze.

Ginger shouted over the crowd's roar, "Mr. Lester looks to be made out of concrete!"

There wasn't an ounce of fat on Sid Lester's body, and his face, replete with a bent nose and crooked mouth, looked like it was carved from granite. Though Marvin looked lean and athletic, the scene was like seeing a small lorry racing towards a steam locomotive. There was little doubt as to what would happen if the two should crash together.

The bell rang. Shouts came from all regions of the crowd and each fighter's corner. Sid Lester had his gloved hands raised to about chest height in front of him, while Marvin's were raised to just below eye level. The two fighters' differences in style were immediately evident, even to a novice to the sport like Ginger. Sid Lester plodded forward like a slow-moving thundercloud, eyes dark and angry, while Marvin stayed in perpetual motion as he lightly danced forwards and side to side on the balls of his feet.

Sid Lester threw the first punch. A collective gasp came from the crowd as his gloved hand sailed over Marvin's head, but Marvin deftly ducked under the left hook and danced to his right.

In return, Marvin delivered a chopping blow to Sid Lester's midsection. The champion didn't seem to notice the abuse. It was like watching someone trying to chop a tree down with a spoon.

Countering with a vicious right, Mr. Lester grazed past Marvin's cheek with his glove, but the youth moved his head to the left just in time. Horrified gasps came from the audience and Ginger as well. Basil stiffened at her side. Ginger was sure the fight would've been over had that punch connected.

The fighters realigned themselves. Mr. Lester seemed heavy-footed, and Marvin looked like he had springs attached to his boots. Marvin shot a straight left jab into the champion's face, causing Mr. Lester's head to snap straight back. Appearing to freeze on the spot, the champion seemed surprised. This was all Marvin needed to deliver a blindingly fast flurry of blows with both hands. Mr. Lester stumbled back against the ropes, only to barrel forward again, throwing left and right punches that seemed awkward compared with Marvin's lightning-fast delivery and evasive manoeuvring. Marvin darted out of the way before anything of any substance could connect.

Ginger couldn't believe what she was seeing.

It was a portent of things to come as the rest of the round progressed, with Marvin delivering highly accurate left jabs while dancing lightly to his left. This rendered the champion's famous left hook almost useless, forcing him to continually turn too far to his right to deliver any real power.

One could see the anger and frustration building in the champion's expression as his swings became wilder, only to connect with space. It was like fighting a zephyr. By the end of the first round, the crowd had grown significantly quieter. So far, the champ had only landed glancing blows while Marvin had scored countless hits to Sid Lester's head and torso.

In the second round, the champion came out like an angry bull. Despite this, Marvin danced backward and moved his head out of harm's way with an almost other-worldy speed and timing.

It was clear the match was not going the way the newspapers had predicted, and Ginger could see by the sour expressions on many a man's face that their bets were in danger.

The same pattern continued for the next three rounds. Mr. Lester got about half a dozen good shots to Marvin's body, but only twice did the champion manage to tag Marvin with a glancing blow to the head.

Marvin seemed able to shrug those off admirably, which was a testament to his conditioning. As time went on, it seemed to Ginger that Marvin gained even more confidence as he studied his opponent's rhythm and got a sense of his weak points. He connected with hooks and uppercuts almost at will, while the champion seemed confused that all his powerful punches were meeting only air. Sid Lester's face was swollen around both eyes, and his upper lip had thickened, while Marvin's face looked untouched.

"I take it this is unexpected," Ginger said.

Basil lifted his flat cap, ran his fingers through his hair, then twisted it back on. "It's shocking. I wouldn't believe it if I weren't seeing this with my own eyes."

Ginger eyed her husband but left the provocative question unspoken. Had this fight been rigged?

Between rounds, the black man in Marvin's corner shouted instructions in his ear. Marvin nodded between gulps of water.

In the champion's corner, Sid Lester furiously pushed away his corner coach, an older man with a shock of white hair and a crooked nose, and an assistant holding out water and a towel.

Then, to everyone's amazement, when the bell rang to start the seventh round, the champion did not rise. Instead, he glared at Marvin with dull resignation. His corner coach rubbed his fighter's shoulder vigorously, causing Lester to grimace in pain. A moment later, Sid Lester's corner coach waved a white flag and threw it into the centre of the ring.

The crowd erupted in boos and shouts of derision. A broad-shouldered man, apparently one of Marvin's lone supporters, caught Ginger and Basil's attention. With a loud gravelly voice, he shouted, "Elliot!"

Marvin jumped up and did a shuffling dance in the middle of the ring, his hands raised high as the announcer entered the ring with his megaphone.

Ginger leaned into Basil. "What's happening?"

"It's over." Basil shook his head, a deep frown on his face. "Marvin is the new middleweight champion of London."

# 3

*O*nce the crowd's outrage settled, individuals, couples, and groups made their way to the exits, grumbling and shaking heads with grim expressions on their faces.

"And here I thought everyone had come for a good time," Ginger quipped.

Basil linked his arm with hers. "Sports betting isn't for the faint of heart."

"Do you think," Ginger started, "that possibly we were just treated to a show?"

Basil put a finger to his lips. "Best to keep your voice down, love. Emotions run high where money is involved, and if suspicion of duplicity became widespread, it could be dangerous for Marvin."

"Oh mercy." Ginger wondered what kind of trouble Marvin had got himself into now. "We should go to him," she added. "To make sure he's all right. He should know that we came to support him."

"I'm afraid they won't let a lady into the dressing rooms."

Moving out of the way of the slow-moving river of spectators pressing towards the doors, Ginger pulled Basil to a stop. "Then you must go."

Basil's eyebrows furrowed. "And leave you here on your own?"

Ginger reassured her husband. "I'm quite able to take care of myself."

"I know that, but regardless, I don't want you to be uncomfortable."

Ginger followed Basil's gaze that scoured the emptying hall. Despite the barbaric nature of the event, the spectators, for the most part, looked upright and respectable, much as Ginger and Basil did. Women were few but not absent, so Ginger wasn't in any danger of being the lone female in the place.

"Go and talk to Marvin," Ginger said. "It'll only take you a few minutes. Just make sure he's truly all right and put my heart at ease."

"Very well, love," Basil conceded. "I shan't be long."

Ginger settled into an empty chair, preparing for the wait. She tucked her red bob behind her ears. As she smoothed her skirt and crossed her legs at the ankle, she admired her Parisian shoes which were textured with gold fabric and had a quilted look. The square heel fanned out, slightly larger than the base, and had a delicate buckle-up strap that crossed the ankle.

Despite her apparent obsession with her footwear, Ginger kept her senses in tune with her surroundings. She'd learned to keep on guard during the war years while working for the British government as a secret agent in France. This skill had now brought awareness of a man across the room who'd made no secret of watching her. He wore an expensive suit with a new trilby on his head and polished leather shoes on his feet. His hooded eyes were dark and brooding, almost birdlike, but perhaps that image came to Ginger because of the man's hawkish nose. In Ginger's opinion, a moustache would've balanced out his features nicely, but the man seemed close friends with his barber, as his hair was trimmed short and his face cleanly shaved.

Ginger groaned inwardly when the man stepped towards her. She looked at her watch—Basil had been gone for ten minutes—then made a point of playing with her wedding ring.

The silent declaration of her marital status didn't prevent the man from claiming the empty chair beside her. As the hall had cleared out and there were plenty of empty seats to choose from, Ginger was forced to presume he'd singled her out.

"I'm waiting for my husband," she said. "He's with the new champion."

"Ah, Marvin the Mouth," the man said. "Or should I say the *Marvellous?* Are you related?"

"And why would you think that?" Ginger wasn't normally so blunt or rude, but something about the man made her uncomfortable. Besides, he was the one being rude, forcing his company on her without invitation.

"You said your husband was with him. It's a natural assumption." His eyes scanned her from hat to Parisian footwear. "You don't look like the type of lady who'd enjoy these kinds of vicious events."

How dare this man make conclusions about her character. "One mustn't judge a book by its cover," she said, then shifted in her seat, facing away from the stranger.

"And yet, you've judged me."

Ginger turned back to face the man. "Can I help you with something, Mr.—"

The man casually got to his feet. "If ever that may be the case, Mrs. Reed, I'll let you know." He tipped his hat, pivoted on the heel of his shoe, and took large strides towards the exit.

Feeling alarmed that the man knew who she was but that the knowledge hadn't been reciprocated, Ginger jumped to her feet. "Wait!"

The man hesitated but didn't turn to her voice. He kept walking until he disappeared amidst a group of late-leaving stragglers.

# 4

There were several changing rooms down a long brick-floored hallway, but when Basil encountered a small crowd of press reporters, he knew he was closing in on Marvin. Jostling through the press members, Basil came to two doors: one with Sid Lester's name attached to it and one with Marvin's.

A surly-looking, barrel-chested man, who could have once been a professional pugilist, stood between the two entrances, his thick arms folded. "Mr. Elliot isn't ready for the press."

"I'm a near relative of Mr. Elliot's," Basil said with authority.

The brawny man grunted and opened Marvin's door. Inside, the smell of sweat and cleaning solution burned Basil's nostrils. Marvin sat on an elevated bench with a towel wrapped around his neck. His corner coach was untying his gloves. Marvin raised a bruised chin in Basil's direction, staring back with the one eye that wasn't swelling shut.

"Mr. Reed!"

"Hello, Marvin," Basil said with a grin. "That was quite a performance."

"All skill, guv." Marvin smiled. "I'm fast on me feet. No old ogre's gonna knock me out."

Marvin spoke quickly, his right knee bouncing up and down, with his heel never touching the ground. His one good eye blinked rapidly, and Basil wondered if Marvin still had adrenaline coursing through his system. Or, he thought soberly, something else? Something artificial?

Basil rubbed his chin as he responded. "You have an entire hall of witnesses to attest to that."

Marvin's assistant pulled off the white tape wrapped around his left hand.

"I didn't see you in the crowd, sir," Marvin said. "Did Mrs. Reed come too?"

"She did."

"Blimey. I wouldn't 'ave expected that."

"She came to offer her support, as did I. In fact, she sent me here to make sure you were all right. Are you?"

With a crooked smile, Marvin said, "Why wouldn't I be?"

Before Basil could answer, Marvin flipped to a new subject. "Now, where are me manners? I'd like you to meet Mr. Willard Shaftoe or 'Wiley' as 'e's known round 'ere." Marvin nodded towards the black corner coach. "Wiley, this 'ere is Chief Inspector Reed from Scotland Yard, 'oo 'appens to be related to me somehow."

"Pleased to meet you, Chief Inspector." The man extended a hand to Basil.

Wiley was solidly built with a slight paunch and greying hair that placed him in his mid-fifties. His voice was resonant but low and raspy when he spoke, like it had been soaked in whisky and cigar smoke for decades.

"Likewise," Basil said, taking the offered hand.

"I wouldn't be 'ere if it weren't for old Wiley 'ere," Marvin said. With the gloves removed, he opened and closed his fists as if to encourage blood to flow through his fingers. "'E came to me when I was trainin' meself in a club in South London and offered me 'is services as a trainer. Wiley used to fight for a club in Croydon. He was district champion twenty years ago."

"Is that so?" Basil said as he cocked his head to consider the trainer.

"Yeah, those days are ancient history and many a drink behind me," Shaftoe said, "But Marvin here, I knew he was going a be a serious contender. But I didn't know we'd be looking at the London title this soon."

"I'd say most of the hall tonight would agree with you, Mr. Shaftoe. I've heard that Sid Lester isn't known for failing to answer the bell." Basil cast a glance

Marvin's way. "Not that you didn't fight superbly, Marvin. Don't get me wrong, but I think—"

"We're just as surprised as everyone else," Marvin said, interrupting. Again, he appeared almost manic in his speech, like he couldn't wait for Basil to finish his sentence. "I knew I could beat 'im. I went to see 'im fight two months ago. 'E's a monster, all right. There's more power in 'is fists than anyone I've seen. But I 'ad 'im figured out easy enough. 'E swings too wide and keeps 'is gloves too low. Someone fast like me can get in and out without getting 'is 'ead knocked off. But . . ." He looked at Basil and shook his head. "It ended too soon. I wish the fight 'ad gone longer."

Basil rubbed the back of his neck. "Judging from the crowd's reaction," he said, "you're not the only one."

Marvin's cheeks flushed with a bout of indignation. "I feel like I've been robbed of some glory 'ere!"

"What do you think, Mr. Shaftoe?" Basil asked.

"His corner said he sustained some kind of shoulder injury." Shaftoe shrugged. "But that ain't how I seen it. Not at all."

Basil leaned in and lowered his voice. "You think he threw the fight?"

"I don't know." Wiley Shaftoe narrowed his eyes in thought. "It was more like he just gave up when he finally realised he couldn't catch Marvin with anything. Sid Lester ain't gone more than five rounds in many years. If the fight had gone longer, he would've started to look like a drunk. I think he might just be getting old and he's too blasted proud to admit it."

"So, he faked the shoulder injury?" Basil said.

"Something like that." The wizened trainer snorted in derision. "Not exactly an honourable exit from a fight."

"I'm curious, Marvin," Basil began. "The press has started labelling you as Marvin the Mouth. You have gained the habit of being outspoken about your opponents. Especially about Sid Lester. You hardly know the man; why did you . . . ?"

"To sell tickets!" Marvin laughed as he used a small towel to wipe new sweat from his forehead. "It's a trick I learned when I started fightin' in the navy. If yer insult yer opponent, yer get all 'is supporters angry and eager for the fight. Far more of 'is lot would show up in anticipation of watchin' 'im shut up the braggart. Works every time." He grinned. "For this fight, I was promised a large percentage of ticket sales."

"Well," Basil said, stepping towards the door. "Congratulations on your win, Marvin. Do take care."

Basil was deep in thought as he exited the dressing room area and stepped into the main hall. Marvin's life was about to change considerably, and a strange set of circumstances had set the whole thing in motion.

After scanning the hall for Ginger's familiar form, he spotted her seated in the front row of a vacated section. The grin that had tugged on his cheeks slid away when he saw a man speaking in her direction.

The well-dressed man was tall, slim, and had sandy-coloured hair he wore slicked back. His profile was birdlike, with a distinguished-looking nose.

Basil's blood froze.

Years in prison had aged him a little, but Mortimer Sharp, otherwise known as The Griffin, was as sinister-looking as he had been on the day he was sentenced to prison on charges of fraud filed over a decade earlier.

Thanks to Basil's efforts, the man had gone down for fraud.

But Basil knew he was guilty of murder.

5

When Basil revealed the name of the man who'd been giving her unwanted attention, Ginger was stunned. She gaped at her husband, one hand on the dashboard of his Austin as he made a sharp turn towards Kensington.

"That was Mortimer Sharp?"

It was a rhetorical question as the tense jawline and pinched skin around Basil's hazel eyes were evidence of the truth of his words.

Ginger brought her lips together as she considered the implications. During the war, she'd found herself in many frightening situations, facing and seeing death plenty of times. The fear that percolated in her belly now, coursed through her being and tingled her spine.

The difference between the war and this man was this: the war wasn't personal. The carnage that happened around her wasn't *because* of her. If something happened to her, it would be considered collateral damage. Faceless soldiers shooting bullets and dropping bombs were fighting for ideals, not to harm her specifically.

Her late husband, Daniel, was the only person she had loved until now, who had been in constant danger. But his whereabouts were usually foggy to her until the end when he'd been betrayed by Captain Smithwick, the leader of his brigade.

She'd thought she was vulnerable then because of him, but that didn't compare with how she felt now. A nemesis could spear her heart, not only through Basil, but baby Rosa, Scout, and the other members of her family whom she loved dearly: Ambrosia, Felicia, and Charles. At least her half-sister, Louisa, and stepmother, Sally, were in Boston, safely out of Mortimer Sharp's reach.

"He knew who I was," Ginger said.

Basil hit the brakes, pulling the motorcar to the kerb and nearly throwing Ginger against the door. Colour drained from his face. "What?"

"He called me Mrs. Reed."

Basil hit the steering wheel with his fist. "Blast it!"

Ginger inhaled, pinching her eyes shut, trying to think. Mortimer Sharp was a kingpin in a known gang. He'd spent the last eleven years in prison because of Basil's detective work. His daughter, Vera, had taken exception to that and had come after Basil's family. Her efforts had ultimately failed.

But now Mortimer Sharp was back.

"Do you believe we're in danger?" Ginger asked.

Basil shook his head as he put the motorcar back into gear. "I don't know. I wasn't the only one responsible for his jail sentence." Entering the roadway behind a double-decker motorbus, he added, "If I'd had my way, he'd have been strung up for murder."

"Vera Sharp is at Broadmoor, alive and well, even if she's insane," Ginger said. "Her father can visit her at any time." Her words were an effort to calm herself down with logic.

"I never got the impression that he cared all that much for her," Basil said. "It's more the principle of the thing."

"Why was he at the fight?" Ginger placed a hand on Basil's sleeve. "Not because of Marvin, I hope."

"It's quite probable that he knows the connection between Marvin and me," Basil said.

Ginger didn't doubt it. The fact that *Marvin the Mouth,* now *Marvin the Marvellous,* was a cousin of the adopted son of Basil and Ginger Reed had become fodder for the rags in recent weeks.

"But," Basil continued, "it's more likely that Sharp was in attendance for the same reason as most other men: He'd bet on the fight."

Ginger was going to revisit Mr. Sharp's knowledge of her identity, but they were halfway down the lane behind Hartigan House, and Basil was about to pull into the garage in the back garden.

Though it was clearly unreasonable, Ginger had an intense urge to see her children, to make sure they were safe, and nearly sprinted down the cobbled path that split the lawn into two sections as she approached the rear entrance of the house. Basil must've felt her concern as he tossed the keys to Clement, the gardener, so he could park the Austin for him and hurried along behind her.

Pippins, Ginger's long-time butler, must've heard the motorcar engine rumbling as he was waiting at the door.

"Madam," he said with a slight bow. Pippins, who was tall once, had lost some height to the curving of his back and shoulders, a common malady of those in advanced age. Ginger had once suggested he retire, continue to live in his quarters at Hartigan House, but give his duties to someone younger. He'd flatly refused.

"I'll come to my end if I do that, my lady," he'd said, using the title she'd gained when she'd married Daniel, Lord Gold.

Pippins held out an arm, accepting her coat.

"Good evening, Pips," Ginger said, followed quickly by, "Are the children upstairs?"

"Indeed, madam. Nanny Green is caring for the baby and Master Scout is in his bed."

Ginger wanted to ask if the butler was sure, but it was hardly Pip's responsibility to ensure the lad went to bed and stayed in his room. She wouldn't breathe easy until she saw the fact for herself.

Pippins and Basil exchanged greetings, joining Ginger as they headed down the corridor to the black-and-white tiled entranceway. But Basil paused under the large electric chandelier instead of following Ginger up the curved staircase.

"I'm stopping in the sitting room, love," he said. "For a nightcap."

"Of course," Ginger returned. "I'll join you shortly. I only want to visit the loo."

Ginger held Basil's gaze briefly, his eyes knowing the truth. As she hurried up the stairs, he said, "I'll have your brandy waiting."

Since Scout's room was closer, Ginger headed there first. The door was cracked open, and a soft light was being emitted into the corridor. Ginger let out a breath as she took in her son, reading with the help of a small electric lamp, and faithful Boss curled at his feet.

"Oh hello, Mum," he said when he saw her. His youthful brow buckled. "Are you all right? You look like you've had a fright."

Ginger patted Boss as she forced a smile. "I'm fine. I was just eager to see you. What are you reading?"

"*Black Beauty*."

Her son couldn't seem to get enough of horses. "Fabulous."

Scout pushed up taller against his pillows. "How did Marvin do?"

The look on his face showed fear for the answer, and Ginger was quick to assuage his worry. "He won."

"He won? He *won?*"

"He did."

Ginger gave her son a quick smile before heading for the window. They were on the first floor above ground, but a masterful climber could scale the limestone and grip the downpipes if he intended to break in. Ginger closed the window and secured the lock.

"Mum?" Scout asked with a questioning side glance.

"It's chilly out tonight," Ginger said.

"I can't believe he won!" Scout relaxed back into his pillows. "Did you talk to him?"

"No, but Dad did. You can ask him about it tomorrow." Ginger stopped to kiss his head. "Now, don't stay up too late reading."

Boss stretched out, exposing his furry belly, and Ginger gave him a playful rub. "Mr. Fulton is coming early in the morning." The tutor had kindly made room for Scout in his summer schedule until the next term at Scout's new "nature school" began. Ginger had learned that the owner of a breeding estate near St. Albans and his scholarly brother were boarding a few students with strong equine interest and aptitude. In Ginger's mind, it was a specialised situation that was an answer to prayer.

Ginger found baby Rosa asleep in her crib. In the adjoining room, Nanny Green sat reading.

"Don't mind me," Ginger said to her. "I'm just saying a quick goodnight to Rosa."

Ginger longed to lift Rosa into her arms, but it would be unfair to the child to wake her. Instead, Ginger stroked the child's fine, dark hair and kissed her soft forehead. She took in a breath of the baby's heady scent. "You're all right. Everyone is all right."

Ginger stopped in her bedroom to brush her hair before joining Basil in the sitting room—a room she loved with its tall windows, Persian carpet, and brick fireplace. A Waterhouse painting, *The Mermaid*, hung above the mantel, a favourite piece of Ginger's as the mystical red-headed beauty brought thoughts of the mother she wasn't blessed to know. She had a much-loved wing-backed chair with an ottoman for resting her feet on but always sat with Basil on the settee when they were lounging together.

Basil handed Ginger a crystal tumbler with a finger's worth of brandy in it. "I take it the children are safe in their beds?" he said.

Ginger seated herself. "You were worried too. Thanks for sending me into the trenches."

"I wasn't worried," Basil insisted, "at least not once I set eyes on Pippins."

Ginger smiled. "Pips does seem to be ever-present and all-knowing."

"At least when it comes to the goings-on in this house."

After a sip of brandy, she said, "Still, I'm

concerned. One could scale the walls and breach the upper-floor rooms if one was inclined."

"Ginger..."

Ginger held up a finger. "It would take five minutes or less." After all, she had scaled a wall in France to escape the Boche.

Basil held her gaze. "Your mind frightens me sometimes."

"Yes, well, perhaps it's not my mind we need to be frightened of at the moment."

"Very well. I'll make some calls in the morning. I'll hire another man."

After their last case, Basil had hired a security man to watch the house, but it seemed superfluous in an area like Mallowan Court, especially once the danger had passed.

But now it had returned.

"Good idea," Ginger said. "At least until we understand what Mortimer Sharp wants."

"He may only want to get on with his life of fraudulent dealings," Basil said. "Speaking to you might've been a warning for me to stay out of his way."

"Perhaps," Ginger said, unconvinced. "I just hope Marvin hasn't got caught up in anything nefarious."

Basil chuckled. "He doesn't have the best track record."

Ginger got to her feet and held out her hand to Basil. Things always seemed more serious at night than they did during the day. Best to go to bed and get a good night's sleep.

"Don't forget that Felicia and Charles are coming for breakfast."

"Righto," Basil said as he stood. Weaving his fingers through Ginger's, he led her upstairs.

# 6

*G*inger's heart expanded every time her family gathered, even if the occasion was simply breakfast. Mrs. Beasley, helped by her kitchen staff, had provided a sideboard of hotplates with eggs, sausages and bacon, black pudding, fried kippers, buttered toast, and marmalade.

Warm summer sun filtered through the rear-facing windows of the morning room, brightening the atmosphere, although the conversation seemed stuck on the boxing match from the evening before.

"Lester was a safe bet," Charles said. The Earl of Witt, known as Lord Davenport-Witt, was Felicia's new husband. A handsome man, Charles was tall with dark hair and blue eyes. "If I were a betting man, I'd have been tempted to bet my life savings."

Felicia, the sister of Ginger's late first husband, was pretty with a short dark bob, bright grey eyes, and a heart-shaped face. With a smile, she placed a dainty hand on Charles' sleeve. "Thank goodness you're not a betting man, or we'd be moving back into Hartigan House."

Ginger laughed at her former sister-in-law. Felicia and her grandmother, Ambrosia—the dowager Lady Gold—had moved in with Ginger shortly after Ginger had returned to London. Ambrosia remained instated.

"Men knocking each other senseless is hardly a sport in my books," the dowager said. The Gold family matriarch had a deeply lined face that testified to life experience Ginger knew she'd rather not admit to. She had round deep-set eyes and grey hair that had grown long enough to pull back into a bun after a much-regretted foray into a shorter modern hairstyle.

"I can't believe Marvin won," Scout said, seemingly oblivious to Ambrosia's intended slight.

He'd gone through several solemn and quiet weeks, and Ginger was happy to see him finally engage in conversation.

"And to think, he's my cousin!"

Ginger didn't miss the look that shot between Basil and Charles. Neither believed Marvin had won on his own merits, and Ginger was inclined to agree; however, now wasn't the time to get into that.

Ginger caught Felicia's eye as the conversation inevitably turned to tennis and cricket. "How are you feeling, my dear?" she quietly asked. "Has your morning health improved?"

Felicia blushed at the implication and pressed her cloth napkin to her lips before nodding. "Yes. The physician says everything is coming along as it should."

Ginger was pleased that little Rosa would have a cousin to grow up with.

Basil's voice pulled her back into the conversation. "It's called an iron lung. I read about it in *The Times*. It's said to help polio sufferers with chest paralysis."

"I read about that too," Ginger said. "Haley must be like a pig in mud with the development."

"Haley?" Charles asked.

"My dear American friend, Haley Higgins," Ginger returned. "She's studying to be a doctor. She lived with Ambrosia, Felicia, and me when she studied at the London School of Medicine for Women."

Scout clasped at his chest. "An iron *lung*?"

"It's not a literal lung, son," Basil said. "It's actually two vacuum cleaners in an iron box, almost the length of a motorcar. It's designed to exert a push-pull motion on the chest."

"Like breathing?" Scout said.

Ginger noticed her son's hand hanging down and Boss nosing the boy's fist. A little treat of sausage or bacon must have been sneaked. Ginger held in her grin. She'd been guilty of such table-side misdemeanours herself.

"The photograph looked more like something one would see in *Metropolis*."

"*Metropolis?*" Ambrosia said. "What on earth is that?"

"It's a film, Grandmama," Felicia explained. "Set in the future."

"The future?" Ambrosia blew heavily through lined lips. "How can one know what will be in the future?"

"It's referred to as *scientifiction*," Ginger replied. "A term coined by writer Hugo Gernsback. There are plenty of books in the genre, but this is the first time it's been set to film. It premiered early this year in Berlin."

Ambrosia huffed. "I'll have nothing to do with anything that comes from Germany. I'm rather surprised at you lot."

"The war is over, Lady Gold," Charles said amiably. "And the film is rather remarkable, with innovative special effects."

"Imagine if we could hear what the characters were saying," Felicia said. "That would certainly be futuristic."

"Though I admired the artistic endeavour," Ginger said, "I was a little put off by how the underworld people were represented. The workers were stupid and manipulated, while the elite solved all the problems."

"But isn't that the case?" Charles said after a sip of tea. "I'm not being facetious, but realistic. The elite have the education, the resources, and the time."

"That doesn't make it right, love," Felicia said.

"I'm not arguing that it's right," Charles said. "Only that it's logical."

"I agree with Uncle Charles," Scout said.

Everyone turned to face the lad, who blushed at the attention.

"I'm just saying I'm a case in point, am I not? Marvin and I were both poor, and the only reason I'm not on the streets and fighting for my life and living like he does is because I'm no longer poor. The elite have helped me."

Ginger fought back the scowl that threatened to take over her face. He was right, of course. Still, she felt compelled to add, "Yes, but good fortune alone isn't always enough. One must also act to make the most of it, and anyone is capable of that."

"Like Marvin?" Scout pressed.

Ginger thought of the crowds at the fight and how many patrons were high society, which she had found surprising. "Marvin has had other opportunities to better his life," Ginger said, leaving out the fact that she'd helped him join the navy to avoid jail time. "But fighting is what he chose."

"He's made a pretty penny, too," Basil said.

Disquieted, Ginger held Basil's gaze. Marvin had no experience in handling large amounts of money. "I hope he's getting sound counsel."

"Do you think he'll fight again?" Felicia asked. "That's a lot of money, but one can't live off it forever."

"He most certainly will fight again," Basil said.

"It'll be in his contract. Others will want to make money off Marvin's back."

Mortimer Sharp's face flashed through Ginger's mind. She placed her knife and fork on her plate, feeling a sudden loss of appetite.

GINGER WAS on her way to Feathers & Flair. She loved calling in for a dose of the shop's enthusiasm and never tired of regularly viewing new designs or ready-made frocks delivered there. But as she parked her Crossley around the corner on Watson Street, her attention was taken by her other business establishment.

The sign above the door read *Lady Gold Investigations*. With the arrival of Rosa and the marriage of Felicia, who had been her assistant while she was unwed, Ginger had barely set foot inside the office. Without thought, she crossed the road, the handkerchief skirt of her late-summer frock blowing gently in the breeze around her calves. Stepping down the short stairwell, she fished the key out of her handbag and unlocked the wooden door. As she entered, the overhead bell rang, announcing her arrival to no one. Stepping through the short vestibule, she switched on the one electric lamp, tossed her handbag onto one of the leather chairs facing her desk, and settled into her chair behind it. Leaning back, she placed her feet on the desk, crossing her ankles as she admired her T-strap shoes.

In the dim light, Ginger took in the empty office. A former cobbler's shop, Ginger had had interior walls removed to enlarge the space and papered the walls with a cream-and-gold art deco print. Her desk was along the left wall as one walked in through the enclosed waiting area, with a second desk where Felicia worked sitting perpendicular. A tall black typewriter rested on that one. Down the narrow corridor was a small kitchen with a gas ring for boiling water for tea or coffee, and behind that, a cleaning cupboard which had been converted into a dark room. Ginger remembered how excited she had been when she'd discovered the space. She'd enjoyed remodelling and decorating it and the thrill of setting up the sign and making her calling cards.

Ginger opened the top desk drawer and picked up a card from the pile inside. With a feeling of melancholy, she held it up and read the inscribed text *Lady Gold Investigations* and underneath, the Watson Street address and the office telephone number.

The work that came her way was mainly domestic or random misdemeanours, and Felicia had become a big help. At first, Ginger had employed her to file, take notes, and make tea and coffee, but soon, Felicia's skills as a mystery writer became useful in more expedient ways.

Ginger let out a long breath. Perhaps it was time to let this business go. She was busy now with Rosa, Scout, and Basil, plus her dress shop. And her sleuthing needs were met with the consultant work she did with Basil and the Metropolitan Police.

Letting the investigative office go made sense, even if it saddened Ginger a little. She lowered her feet to the floor. After searching her address book for the landlord's telephone number, she lifted the receiver and was about to relay the number to the operator when the doorbell rang. Steps were heard in the vestibule. A knock sounded on the interior door.

"Hello?"

Ginger stood. "Hello? May I help you?"

The woman wore a navy-blue, slender-fitting suit dress with low heels. Her straight dark hair was cut in a stark bob. She pierced Ginger with a dark-eyed stare.

"Do you remember me?" she asked in French.

Ginger startled as recognition dawned. "*Oui*," Ginger returned. Her mind flashed to a fiery scene in the middle of a Belgian forest. The woman before her had been a fearless member of the Belgian secret service. Together they had burned a German telephone exchange hut to the ground. In English, she asked, "Do you still go by Magna?"

"Yes. Magna Jones."

Ginger doubted that either name had been assigned to her at birth.

"And you?" Magna returned without a trace of a French accent. "I see you've dropped Antoinette La Fleur. Are you really a 'Lady'? Or is that a matter of convenience?"

"My late husband was a baron," Ginger said. "I officially became Lady Gold when I married him in 1913."

Magna raised a dark brow. "You were nobility during the war?"

"The war had a way of erasing the classes," Ginger said. "At least temporarily."

"Did your husband die in the field?" Magna asked.

Ginger nodded.

"And you remarried a policeman."

Ginger wasn't surprised that Magna Jones knew about her life, and she felt on uneven footing, not knowing anything about her old colleague.

"Forgive my manners," she said. "Please have a seat. I'll make us a pot of tea. Or would you prefer coffee?"

Ginger removed her handbag from the nearest chair, and Magna Jones accepted the proffered seat. "Coffee if it's made the European way. Otherwise, tea shall do."

"I can make strong coffee," Ginger said. "Please excuse me for a moment."

Ginger disappeared into the small kitchen area and lit the gas ring. While she waited for the water to boil, she scooped grounds into the percolator basket. Her mind raced as she tried to make sense of this unexpected visitor after so much time had passed. Magna had lost her entire family to the Boche, and she had taken challenging assignments with the courage of someone with nothing to lose. With the chances Magna had taken, and the danger she'd willingly walked into, Ginger was surprised she had survived the war.

Once the coffee had percolated, Ginger poured two cups, placed them on a tray along with a small bowl of sugar, and returned to her visitor.

"I'm afraid I don't have any milk," Ginger said.

"That's all right," Magna said, accepting her cup. "I take it black."

Ginger added a heaping teaspoon of sugar to hers, stirred it, then returned to her chair on the other side of her desk.

"Miss Jones," she started.

"Magna, please."

"You must call me Ginger."

"Ginger? Is that your Christian name?"

"It's Georgia. After my father, George. My mother gave me the nickname." Ginger pointed to her hair. "Because of the red."

Magna glanced about the office. "It pleased me when I learned you'd opened an investigative office." Her eyes settled on Ginger. "Also a Regent Street dress shop *and* you have a family. You've done very well."

"Thank you," Ginger said cautiously. "You've done your homework."

Magna chuckled. "You are frequently in the society pages. It wasn't hard."

"You have an advantage as I know nothing about you," Ginger returned. "What brings you to London?"

A shadow crossed Magna's face. "Too many bad memories in Belgium. I tried to keep busy to prevent overthinking, but as the years passed, it's become more difficult to find enough to do to succeed." She sipped her coffee. "I thought a change would do me good."

Ginger could understand completely. If she were truly honest with herself, she kept herself busy with work and family for the same reason. It helped her to forget regrettable things that had happened during the war.

"You never married?" Ginger asked.

Magna shook her head. "There were men over the years, but it seems I'm too strong a woman for any of them to last long."

"I'm pleased you decided to look me up," Ginger said after a sip of her sweet, strong coffee. "It's serendipitous that you found me here. I haven't been coming to this office very often."

"I suppose not," Magna said.

Something flashed in the former spy's eye, and Ginger knew this meeting wasn't by chance. Magna had been following her.

Frowning, Ginger asked, "Is there something in particular that you wanted from me?"

Magna set her cup on the desk. "Actually, there is. I'd like you to employ me." She waved at the office. "It's clear you'll need to shut operations down if you don't have some help."

Ginger couldn't help but smile a little. "Are you a mind reader too?"

"You don't need supernatural abilities to make deductive conclusions."

"Well, in fact, I was just about to ring the landlord to cancel my lease."

"Are you certain you want to do that?"

"I was," Ginger said. "But perhaps I was being a little hasty. Tell me, why do you want to work for me, of all people?"

"I need a job. You know my capabilities already. And I bore easily. I crave interesting work. I can't bear to take another receptionist's job."

"It's been pretty boring around here lately."

"You can't take on work when the office door is always locked and there's no one here to answer the telephone."

"Why don't you start your own investigative office?"

"I'd have to start from scratch, and I have no contacts in London."

"I see," Ginger said and took a sip of coffee.

Most people didn't know about Magna's contributions to helping the allies win the war. And she certainly didn't deserve to be unassisted and forgotten. If this was what Magna wanted, and it was in Ginger's power to give it to her, then she would do it.

Ginger had once trusted Magna with her life and found that she trusted her still. Who better to watch over her investigative business than a former elite secret service agent?

"All right. You're hired. I do hope you won't be bored here too." She pointed to Felicia's empty desk. "You can set yourself up there. Come back tomorrow and we'll discuss the particulars."

"*Merci beaucoup*," Magna said. She remained expressionless, though her dark eyes did flash with gratitude.

Ginger smiled. "Welcome to Lady Gold Investigations."

# 7

It'd been a slow week at the Yard, which Basil had used as an excuse to come in later that day than usual. The pile of paperwork on his desk that had greeted him was now nearly whittled down to nothing. He let out a frustrated grunt, mumbling under his breath that he hadn't joined the Met to shuffle papers, but one had to take the good with the bad.

A tap at the door was a welcome distraction until Basil saw Morris standing there, a smug look on his heavy-set face. The superintendent was a pain in the *derrière* on a good day.

"Better put your hat on, Reed," the super said. "There's been a murder in the East End, and you're next up to head the investigation. The pathologist is on his way and will meet you there."

Basil pushed the remaining papers aside. A murder

would certainly make things more interesting. "Yes, sir. Is there any other information?"

"Sports celebrity shot leaving one of those clubs about an hour ago. A bullet blast. Could be gang related. I swear those thugs are making London start to feel like Italy."

"Sports celebrity, sir?"

"Yes, yes, yes." Morris consulted a note in his hand. "A famous London boxer named Sid Lester. I heard the poor bloke lost a fight last night."

Basil froze. "Sid Lester?"

"You look surprised." Morris slipped the note back into his pocket. "Do you know the man?"

Basil shook his head. "Just by reputation, sir."

Mentioning that Sid Lester having recently fought his son's cousin seemed imprudent, especially since he had been taken off a recent case due to a conflict of interest through familial ties. Of course, it was too early for any suspect list, and Basil didn't believe Marvin could be involved in Lester's death; however, he felt it best to hold his tongue.

Before long, Basil stood at the rear entrance to the club. Street constables had roped the area off, keeping nosy parkers at bay. The supine form of Sid Lester lay in the dirt close to the building, his face covered with a handkerchief and his blood splattered along the brown brick wall. Basil motioned to Braxton, his usually assigned constable, to follow him.

Dr. Gupta, a handsome Indian man with copper

brown eyes, had beaten Basil to the scene and was crouched low doing a preliminary examination.

"Good day, Doctor," Basil said, announcing his arrival

The pathologist rose. "Good day, Chief Inspector," he returned, then added to Braxton, "Hello, Constable."

Braxton, holding a pencil over a small notebook, nodded back. "Sir."

Gupta motioned to the victim. "Male, about thirty-five years old, in good physical condition."

"Sid Lester," Basil said. "He's a professional fighter."

"Ah," Gupta said with a nod. "That explains things."

"Explains what?" Basil prompted.

"The damage to his fists, the contusions on his ribs, abdomen, and face. Missing teeth. Abuse not related to his cause of death."

Basil didn't have to ask what that was. Two bullet wounds were visible across his chest. Basil shook his head at the damage. A thick river of crimson led from the body to the edge of the pavement and into the street.

Basil had only seen the man in press pictures and then in person at the match. He had always been shirtless and wearing boxing attire. To see him dressed formally, wearing a white shirt, black trousers, and shiny Oxford shoes, was rather striking.

They were approached by a young constable wearing the quintessential navy-blue uniform with a rounded helmet perched on his head and a chinstrap not quite under the chin. "Constable Nolan, sir. I was the first to get 'ere and send word to the Yard. I was just round the corner when I 'eard the shots."

"This is your beat?" Basil asked.

"Yes, sir."

Basil lifted his chin. "Did you hear anything else? See anything suspicious?"

"Three gunshots then the screechin' of tyres, sir. When I got 'ere the owner, Mr. Chandler, an' one of the door supervisors were there. They 'ad both 'eard the same thing I did and come runnin' out."

Basil turned to Braxton. "Go with Constable Nolan to canvass the area. See if you can put together a list of witnesses. With a shooting in broad daylight, someone must've heard or seen something."

"Yes, sir," Braxton said, his notebook at the ready.

"Three shots," Basil said, staring at the lone bullet hole on the exterior wall behind the body. He plucked a casing off the ground. "A forty-five."

"Naturally, I haven't done an autopsy yet," Dr. Gupta said, "but it's clear that one of the bullets pierced the man's heart. He probably died instantly."

"I'll get someone to take some photographs before ambulance services arrive," Basil said.

Gupta snapped his medical bag closed. "My work here is done. I'll await the body at the mortuary."

"Very good," Basil said. "Thank you, Doctor."

Leaving the fallen body of Sid Lester under the watch of two street constables, Basil looked down both ends of the alley. Northward, it ended in a brick wall. South emptied onto Old Ford Road, which went roughly east and west. The police had barricaded the intersection.

Walking to the brick wall and then back to the barricades, Basil scanned the area for clues. Fresh tyre marks curved in the direction out of the alley onto Old Ford Road heading east. Basil scribbled in his notepad starring Sergeant Scott's name, a reminder that the police photographer should take photographs of the skid marks.

There wasn't much to see looking east on Old Ford Road, but Basil knew the area well enough to know that there were no major intersections until the road passed over Regent's Canal and crossed Grove Road. The getaway car would have had few obstacles while fleeing the scene. This was not an area that would attract pedestrians or even other motorcars, and almost a perfect scenario for a quick shooting and a getaway.

Whoever killed Sid Lester knew what they were doing.

Just as Basil stepped away from the barricade on his way back to the crime scene, he heard a familiar voice call out.

"Chief Inspector Reed!"

Basil turned to see Blake Brown, a reporter for *The*

*Daily News*, walking quickly up to the barricade and the on-duty constable, who stopped Mr. Brown before he could get too close. Dressed in wrinkled trousers, he had a satchel strapped diagonally over his waistcoat, a weathered trilby on his head, and the perpetual chewed-on pencil tucked behind his ear. In his right hand, he carried a collapsible Kodak Eastman press camera. "You're surely not going to stop a gentleman of the press, are you?" Brown said, his eyes bright with ambition. "I heard there's been a shooting."

"Brown," Basil said, a scowl forming on his face as he nodded at the constable to let the reporter pass.

Brown stepped in beside Basil. "Thank you, sir."

"If I could stop you without making a fuss, I would," Basil returned. "Can I trust you not to broadcast this all over the neighbourhood just yet? This is still a crime scene."

Brown grinned. "On my honour. How's the missus, by the way?" His eyes darted about the scene. "No Lady Gold? I'm surprised."

"She's rather busy with the family these days," Basil said, leaving out his thoughts that Ginger would jump into this case with the zeal of a pig in mud once she learned of it.

Sergeant Scott was busy taking photographs with a French Furet camera, the flash causing white spots to dance in Basil's peripheral vision.

"Blimey," Blake Brown said as he neared the body. "That's Sid Lester!" He lifted his camera with both hands to snap pictures, but Basil stepped in his way. "Hold on, Brown. Show a little respect. Only the scene for now. No corpse."

The ambulance arrived, nosing into the alley entrance and waiting for the on-duty street constables to move the body for them. Basil stepped closer to the reporter to let the ambulance go by.

Brown raised his brow as the ambulance attendants loaded the covered body onto a stretcher. "I can snap this, can't I?"

Basil nodded, certain that the journalist had plenty of photographs, like those he was taking now, an unidentifiable body shielded by a blanket. The light of the camera's flash illuminated the dark red brick of the hall's outside walls.

"Looks like I got here just in time," Brown said as the ambulance drove away.

"How did you get here so fast?" Basil asked. "The press hasn't been alerted."

"I have my sources."

Basil huffed, wondering which police officer Brown had in his back pocket.

Blake Brown put away his camera and claimed the chewed pencil from his ear, poising its dulled tip over a well-used notepad.

"Any suspects yet, Chief Inspector?"

"You know I can't talk about any of that." Annoyed, Basil turned to walk into the hall.

Brown hurried after him. "Perhaps it's related to all

the gang activity surrounding Lester?"

With his gloved hand on the door handle, Basil pivoted on his heel. "What do you mean?"

"I take it you've not spent much time getting to know the local boxing scene," Brown said.

"Only what I read about it in the papers, and I was at Sid Lester's last match."

"Ha! That was quite a match, all right. No one saw that one coming, I'd wager. Anyway, I've covered Sid Lester's career since he first won the London championship eight years ago. I've interviewed him several times or tried to, anyway. The man was not an easy subject to interview. Not very forthcoming and constantly in a bad mood. I always got the feeling that he would rather strike me on the chin than give me a statement."

"Well, since you seem to know so much about him, perhaps my first interview should be with you," Basil said.

The reporter adjusted his hat and straightened his tie. "I'd be happy to be an interviewee. I help you; you help me, see? Tit for tat."

Basil let go of the door and stepped back into the alley. "All right, I'll bite. Who do *you* think shot Sid Lester?"

"I don't know who, but I would bet it has something to do with those connections I mentioned. Sid Lester was known to associate himself with some unscrupulous individuals."

"Such as?"

"For reasons concerning my safety, I would rather not get into mentioning too many names."

"Now look who is not forthcoming," Basil noted.

"Look, Chief Inspector, I value my skin just as much as the next man. I will leave the naming of names to you on this one, but I can tell you that Sid Lester didn't just throw his fists in the ring. Rumour has it that as recently as just a few years ago, he worked for certain people as a debt collector for some of the cocaine rings here in London."

Basil immediately thought of Marvin and the unusual mannerisms he'd displayed after the fight with Sid Lester.

"Cocaine rings? Since the 1920 Dangerous Drugs Act was passed, only medical practitioners can dispense things like cocaine and morphine," Basil said.

"Yes, but certain criminal elements, sniffing money to be made, have sought to gain control of some doctors and chemists by bribing them or forcing them to do their bidding."

"Scotland Yard would be interested in knowing who those doctors and chemists are." Basil looked at Blake Brown expectantly.

"Sorry, don't have that kind of information."

"Of course not." Basil scowled.

Though he didn't want to show his hand to Brown, the Yard was aware that illegal importation of certain drugs and pharmaceuticals went on, mainly coming from France, and that the centre of such operations was said to be based in Soho and London's East End. But to Basil's knowledge, these were limited operations due to severe police measures in recent years.

"So, you're saying Sid Lester's death is connected with cocaine?"

"Cocaine, sports betting, fraud," Brown answered. "Take your pick. I'm saying that brigands and cheats surrounded Sid Lester, some of whom were powerful men. I bet Sid Lester fell out of favour with one or several of them. Apparently, a dangerous thing to do."

Basil and Blake Brown both looked down at the bloodstain on the ground.

"What do you know about Mortimer Sharp?" Basil asked. "Otherwise known as 'The Griffin'?"

Brown stepped back as something dark flashed behind his curious eyes.

"Hey, like I said, I don't name names." He flicked his wrist as if he intended to check the time, something he didn't actually do, then clicked his tongue. "Look at that. Time flies when you're having fun. Sorry, but I've got to go. I'll see you around, Chief Inspector."

With that, Brown hurried away, a pencil tucked behind one ear, one hand grasping his satchel, and the other holding on to his hat.

Basil didn't doubt that the two would cross paths again, but the confident story-hunter didn't fool him. Blake Brown feared Mortimer Sharp.

# 8

Constable Braxton met Basil as he stepped inside the boxing hall.

"I've almost finished questioning everyone remaining, sir," Braxton said. "There aren't that many. The caretaker, three people watching a sparring match between two up-and-coming middleweight fighters, and the two fighters themselves. I was just about to speak to the manager."

"Are you saying there was a fight going on during the time of the murder?"

Braxton adjusted his helmet. "Yes, sir. It wasn't a publicised match, just an exhibition. Two younger lads from rival boxing clubs fight for six rounds. I'm told there were about fifty spectators."

"Did you learn anything of note?"

"I'm afraid not, sir. Apparently, the sound of the

gun shots outside the brick walls was covered up by the din in here."

Basil lifted his chin. "What about Sid Lester? Did anyone see him leave?"

"Everyone I interviewed was focused on the match. I was just about to talk to the manager. He might know."

"I'll go and see the manager myself," Basil said. "The caretaker and the others can go for now. If they were in the building during the murder, they can't very well have shot anyone outside. We have their names if we need to find them."

Basil found the club manager sitting in a sparsely decorated office. Several pictures of pugilists adorned the brick wall. Various trophies needing dusting sat on a series of shelves.

A sturdy bull-necked man in his early sixties, the manager raised the bushy eyebrows on his high forehead. He looked wary with thinning hair and icy blue eyes.

"Can I help you?" he asked gruffly.

Basil presented his identification. "Chief Inspector Basil Reed from the Yard."

"Ah, I saw your bobbies wandering round."

"And your suspicion wasn't aroused, Mr.—?"

"Friar." The man rose to his feet. "Thomas Friar. And no. Bobbies wander about here more often than you might realise, Chief Inspector. 'Specially the beat coppers. More exciting here than out in the cold, I imagine. Some even jump in the ring, but don't expect me to blow the whistle on them."

Basil smiled amiably, then sobered. "Are you aware there's been a death in the alley just outside the club's back door?"

"Ah, I see. That's what all the hubbub's about, then. I watched some of the match—these young whippersnappers are gonna take the boxing world by storm, you just wait an' see—then I came back here. More deuced paperwork than you can shake a fist at. Worst part of my job."

"The dead man is Sid Lester."

The meaty man blew a breath, then lowered himself into his chair. "You don't say."

Basil slipped his notepad and pencil from his pocket. "You don't seem surprised."

Friar lifted a beefy shoulder. "You know these fighters. Get themselves into hot water sometimes."

"What kind of hot water?"

"I don't know." Friar planted his elbows on his desk and threaded his fingers together. "People bet big money sometimes. What Lester did last night—" He clicked his tongue. "I don't know what he was thinking."

Basil pulled up an empty wooden chair and sat. "I would think this is the last place a fighter would want to be the day after a big fight. Especially a controversial one. What was he doing here? Did he come to watch the exhibition match?"

Friar turned his thick neck. "Lester didn't care about up-and-comers or anybody but himself. He was here to collect his fee for the fight last night."

"Is that normal procedure?" Basil asked. "To collect the fees at the club the next day?"

"Depends on the club, I s'pose. But that's how we do it."

"When did he arrive, exactly?"

"I didn't look at my pocket watch, but it was about halfway through the exhibition."

"Did he say anything to you?"

Friar scowled. "Like what?"

"Anything out of the ordinary," Basil said. "Did he explain why he stopped fighting?"

"Nope. He was tight-lipped. In and out."

"Do you and he get along?"

Friar scoffed. "I don't need to be friends with the fighters. This is business, straight and simple."

"But—"

"Lester was complicated. Complicated the club."

Basil lifted his chin. "How so?"

"I didn't like the company he kept, and I told him so."

"But surely you enjoyed the attention that he brought to your club."

"Yes, at first. But then he started attracting the wrong kind of attention."

Friar folded his arms, his biceps bulging under his

shirt, and Basil couldn't help but admire the strength of a man his age.

"I try to instil a sense of decency and respect in my fighters. Sid Lester had that at one time, but then he got nasty. I tried to warn him off that bad crowd, but he wouldn't listen. I told my other fighters to stay clear of Lester and his gang."

"His gang?"

"You must know, the crowd he was part of." Friar held a finger to his nose and sniffed, giving Basil an obvious hint of their drug use. "They're all filthy gangsters."

"Yet you kept Lester in the club."

Friar snorted. "He kept winning."

Basil tapped his pencil on his notepad. "How about Mortimer Sharp?"

"Mortimer who?"

"Sharp . . . otherwise known as The Griffin. A tall, slim, well-dressed man with a hawkish-looking nose."

"Saw a man like that at the fight with Marvin Elliot last night. Yeah, I know him. Stay clear when I can. He's bad news. A wolf wanting to eat up my fighters."

"Drugs?" Basil asked.

Friar nodded, a vein in his large neck bulging. "Though he'd deny it from here to heaven. I try to protect the lads how I can."

"Can you think of anyone who might've wanted to kill Sid Lester?"

"Hah!" Friar barked. "I imagine everyone from his

corner trainer to his grandmother if she were still alive. Good luck trying to narrow that list down. Lester was a nasty, angry man. He had no friends."

Basil couldn't hold in his surprise. All the photographs in the rags of Sid Lester had other men and women hanging on and around the fighter as if they were the best of friends and lovers.

Friar leaned back in his chair, continuing, "Take Marvin Elliot, for example."

Basil held his breath. On a professional level, he was eager to hear the dirt on Marvin. But personally, he'd rather not.

"What about Elliot?" he asked cautiously.

"He was in a lather at Lester for quitting so early in the fight, and rightly so. I'm furious with the idiot."

"Why do you think he quit?" Basil asked.

"Ego. Plain and simple. He was being made a fool of in the ring an' didn't like it. I can't remember him going over five rounds for as long as I've seen him fight. Always knocked the other guy out cold before that. Elliot was giving him too much in the ring. Lester couldn't risk losing, so he faked a shoulder injury."

"You can confirm it was fake?" Basil asked.

Friar huffed. "I can't. I ain't no doctor. But that's what his corner is saying."

"Did he look like he had a sore shoulder today when he came to pick up his pay?"

"Nope. And I wasn't the only one to notice. Elliot did too."

Basil furrowed his brow. "Marvin Elliot was here this afternoon?"

"After winning like that?" Friar said. "Of course. Poor as a church mouse until last night. Bad timing to run into Lester doing the same thing."

"They had words?" Basil asked.

"A blasted row! Elliot accused Lester of throwing the fight. Told him to his face he could've beat him fair and square. Lester laughed, and Elliot called him a coward. Whoa. Lester's face grew red as a blasted tomato, and I thought I was going to have to break up a fight ring here in my own office."

Friar's neck vein pulsed. "Elliot's not the brightest lad and don't know when to quit. He kept yelling nonsense . . . that Lester was going to pay for robbing him of his big moment. Lester kept his cool and just held out his hand for the money. I handed it over, and he left without so much as a grunt. The miserable sod."

"Did you see Marvin Elliot after that again?"

"Just his tail leaving the club."

"Front door or back?"

"Front. Lester left through the back right afterwards. I watched them both leave cos I didn't want any trouble. I caught the last bit of the exhibition fight."

"I have to ask you this, Mr. Friar. Can anyone confirm your presence at the match when the shooting would have taken place?"

"You think I went out there and shot him?" Friar rolled his eyes.

Basil stared back, saying nothing.

"I don't know," Friar said. "I hung back. Like I said, I was making sure those two nitwits left my club."

Basil stood, slipping his notes into his jacket pocket. "Thanks for your time, Mr. Friar. I'll keep in touch."

Basil's mind raced as he left the building. One bitter thought overshadowed the rest: he was now forced to consider Marvin Elliot as a suspect in the murder of Sid Lester.

## 9

After breakfast, Ginger spent time in the nursery with Rosa, then caught up on her work at her desk in the study. Mostly paperwork—bill paying and collecting, clothing and fabric orders, and opening the post, which naturally led to time sipping tea while perusing the pages of the latest in fashion magazines, her favourite being *Vogue*. This month's edition had autumn-inspired artwork that showed a close-up of a woman wearing an orange cloche hat, poised to eat grapes. The headline was "Early Autumn Fashions & Fashions for Children", the latter being a new interest for Ginger.

She was grateful to have such efficient staff members. Her shop, Feathers & Flair, practically ran without her. And now, her second business, Lady Gold Investigations, had Magna Jones to take care of matters.

Pippins knocked on the door, then entered with a

vase of purple passion flowers in his gloved hands. "Clement picked these from the gardens, madam. I thought perhaps you would enjoy them here."

Ginger stepped out from behind her desk to receive the offering. "Oh, Pips, they're delightful." She sniffed the blossoms, enjoying the sweet fragrance. "But you know who would enjoy these? Lady Davenport-Witt."

"As you wish, madam," Pippins said. "There are plenty more where those came from. Would you like me to have them delivered?"

"No. I'll take them, thank you."

Pippins ducked his chin, then left Ginger alone. It was a warm late-summer day, so no coat or gloves were necessary. Felicia had been rather quiet around the breakfast table, and Ginger had been looking for an excuse to call on her.

Crossing Mallowan Court, Ginger approached what was now referred to as Witt House. She used the wrought-iron knocker, and Burton, Charles' faithful butler, soon opened the door. It had taken the man some time to conform to his changed status in his master's life and the introduction of a new mistress, but he and Felicia had eventually adjusted to each other.

"Good day, Mrs. Reed," he said, standing straight with both hands behind his back

"Good day. Is Lady Davenport-Witt available to see guests? Do apologise for my calling in without an invitation."

"I shall announce you," Burton said. He extended one arm. "Shall I carry the flowers for you?"

Ginger handed the vase over. "That would be splendid."

Despite Ginger's close relationship with Felicia, certain proprieties were expected. As she waited for Felicia, Ginger took time to appreciate the drawing room, now brighter, with fashionable electric lamps and new paint. Much improved from its former state.

Burton returned. "Lady Davenport-Witt will see you. She's in the sitting room and asks you to join her there."

Following Burton, Ginger entered the sitting room to find Felicia stretched out on the sofa, propped up by a fat cushion.

"Don't get up," Ginger said. "It's rude of me to come uninvited."

"Pish-posh!" Felicia said with a flick of her fingers. Then, with her eyes on the blossoms she said, "Are those for me?"

"Yes," Ginger said, taking a chair. "Compliments of Clement."

"How kind." Felicia pointed to the fireplace mantel. "Place them there for now, Burton. Thank you."

The butler did as bid, then asked, "Should I have tea brought in?"

"That would be lovely," Felicia replied.

Once the butler had left, Felicia raised a brow in question. "Is everything all right, Ginger?"

"I was about to ask you the same thing," Ginger returned. "You were awfully quiet at breakfast. Do you feel unwell?"

"No, that part has passed. Thankfully. It's just..."

Ginger grew alarmed as Felicia's eyes brimmed with tears. She reached over and took Felicia's hand. "Love, what is it?"

"It's just, I don't want to sound ungrateful because I know having a child was such a long wait for you, but I'm just not ready." She locked glossy eyes with Ginger. "I'm not ready to be a mother."

"You must've known that since your wedding night. This was always a risk," Ginger said gently.

"Yes, but I followed Marie Stopes' advice, you know, from her book, *Wise Parenthood: a Book for Married People*. These are modern times. There are ways to prevent this, and yet..."

"Felicia, this is why mother nature gave us nine months to adapt. You shall certainly feel differently when the time comes. But for now, enjoy your free time. Don't think about it too much."

"I suppose so," Felicia said, sounding unconvinced.

The maid Daphne arrived, placed a tea tray on the table, and curtsied. "Mrs. Compton has made ginger biscuits. They're fresh out of the oven."

For a change of subject, Ginger regaled Felicia with tales of Rosa's cute antics and Boss' continued adoration of Scout. At one point, she even had her former sister-in-law laughing.

"Oh, Ginger," Felicia said with a smile. "You're such a good friend."

"As are you."

Ginger and Felicia hadn't always got along. When they first met, Felicia was a child of ten and resented Ginger for taking Daniel's heart. Even though Daniel had plenty of love to share, Felicia wasn't warm to the arrangement. Only once Felicia had become an adult and Ginger a widow had they grown close.

Still, Ginger found the subject of friendships a tad unsettling. Apart from within her own family, Ginger hadn't forged any meaningful friendships in London. Not that she wasn't the friendly sort. Everyone who met her knew that she was, but her heart was a deep well, and Ginger protected it.

Her only true friend beyond family was Haley. Oh, how she missed her American friend and longed to see her again. Drat that expansive body of water known as the Atlantic. They were faithful letter writers, but it was natural that distance and time would push them apart. She let out a soft sigh.

"Oh," Felicia said. "Am I boring you?"

"Not at all." Ginger chuckled. "My mind wandered for a moment there. I hope you're feeling better?"

Felicia smiled. "I am. Thank you for coming over."

Ginger squeezed Felicia's hand before she left.

"You're going to be a great mother, Felicia. And I think you'll like being a mum."

BY THE TIME Ginger returned to Hartigan House, Scout had finished his daily lessons. They had a delightful lunch together on the patio in the back garden—a lovely spread of ham and tomato sandwiches, a selection of cheeses, and strawberries and cream—with Scout and Ginger slipping bits of meat to Boss, who was strategically between their two chairs. The meal ended with the surprise arrival of Basil motoring towards the garage in his Austin. He parked in front of the door in a manner that told Ginger he didn't plan on staying long.

"Darling!" Ginger called out. "We weren't expecting you so soon. Is everything all right?"

"Yes, absolutely fine," Basil said jovially.

But something in his eyes made Ginger think that because of Scout's presence, her husband was making light of whatever had brought him home.

"Hello, Dad," Scout said before giving Basil a description of how he and Mr. Fulton had taken the horses for a ride through Kensington Gardens.

"That's fantastic, son," Basil said. "Now, why don't you go inside and wash? I need a few minutes with your mother."

Scout whistled for Boss, and the dog followed him inside.

"I'm nervous," Ginger said. "What's happened?"

"Sid Lester is dead. Shot in the alley behind the boxing club. I wanted you to hear it from me."

"Oh mercy." Ginger rose as she motioned for Basil to take Scout's vacated chair. "I'll have Mrs. Beasley prepare you some lunch." Ginger relayed her request to one of the maids and then rejoined Basil. "Now, I want to hear everything."

"When Morris designated me to take the lead, I had no idea who the victim was; I only knew that it was a shooting. I was stunned to hear Sid Lester was the victim."

"As am I," Ginger said. "You've been to the scene already, I presume. What did you find there?"

"Three shots had been fired. The copper on the beat said he heard the squeal of tyres. I walked to the alley. The killer must've been waiting in a parked motorcar at the dead end, expecting Lester to leave the club."

"So, he had to have known Lester was inside and about what time he would depart," Ginger said. "Someone privy to his private schedule."

"When Lester stepped into the alley, the driver sped up and shot as he raced by."

"Could this be accomplished by one man?" Ginger selected a piece of Cheddar cheese. "The driver's side being on the right of the machine in this country." Ginger had learned to drive in America, so the distinction was important to her.

"Possible but difficult," Basil said. "One would have to operate the machine while shooting and aiming to kill. My guess is there was more than one person involved. Likely a group."

"You mean a gang," Ginger said huskily. Mortimer Sharp's face came to mind, and her heart skipped a beat.

The maid brought Basil his lunch, set it on the table, then curtsied. "Is there anything else you need, sir? Madam?"

"That will be all, Grace," Ginger said. "Thank you."

"To answer your question about gangs," Basil started, "perhaps, but not necessarily." He took a bite of a crisp cucumber sandwich triangle. "Though Thomas Friar did mention gangs and a bad crowd."

"Who's Thomas Friar?"

"The owner of the club. You probably saw him on the night of the fight. A stocky fellow, balding, bushy eyebrows . . ."

"Oh yes. Strutted about with a big grin and steel blue eyes."

"That's him. He didn't hide his dislike for Lester."

"Did he dislike him enough to kill him?" Ginger asked.

"I don't know how he could have done it, to be honest. He would've had to leave the club before Lester, run down the alley, rev up the motorcar, and race down the alley whilst shooting."

"He could've been working with someone."

"My thoughts exactly. He put on a good show of portraying himself as a man who didn't appreciate or tolerate the criminal element."

"You don't believe him?"

Basil chuckled. "I don't believe anyone other than you, my love."

Ginger smiled. "It's hard to believe the best in people in this business."

"Indeed. I'm also starting to believe that drugs have entered this sport."

"To enhance performance?" Ginger said. "Like what?"

"Cocaine, probably. Perhaps other stimulants."

"I've read that it's becoming a problem in all sorts of sporting activities," Ginger said. "People are willing to cheat to win." She pursed her lips, displeased. "I just don't understand."

Basil nibbled on a piece of cheese. "When money is involved, scruples go out of the window."

"What about Marvin?"

Basil paused, holding her gaze. "What about him?"

"Is he using drugs?" Basil had told Ginger about Marvin's odd, hyperactive behaviour, and she'd witnessed it when Marvin was in the ring. "Is he safe?"

Basil took a sip of tea, then cocked his head. "The answer to both is, 'I don't know'. But I do mean to talk to him right after this."

Ginger sprang to her feet. "I'm coming with you. Just give me ten minutes to get ready."

Basil laughed. "I wouldn't imagine it otherwise."

MARVIN LIVED in a rundown boarding house in the East End, not far from Bethnal Green. Once a grand family house, it had been converted into several bedsits over the years. The exterior showed neglect, with overgrown vines scaling the walls, sooty-looking brick, and peeling paint on the windowsills.

The main door was opened by a boarder leaving the house, allowing Ginger and Basil to enter. A person singing "Ain't Misbehavin'" off-key could be heard through the corridor. Ginger knew the number of Marvin's room and knocked on the scratched-up wooden door. When Marvin failed to answer, Basil followed up with three hard raps with his knuckle.

"Marvin?" he called. "It's Mr. and Mrs. Reed. We'd like to talk."

A curse word and the shuffling of feet were heard on the other side of the door. Then the handle turned, the door swung open, and there stood Marvin. His hair was messy, and his tattered dressing gown was loosely tied, revealing a youthful and well-formed chest.

"Good day, Scout's new mum and dad! This's a surprise, innit?" With exaggerated arm movements, he waved them inside. "Come in, come in!"

An unmade bed took up one corner, with a well-used wooden table and two chairs in another. In contrast to the shabby surroundings, an expensive bottle of gin sat half empty on the table, explaining Marvin's apparent early-evening intoxication. A new bowler hat and trench coat hung on the coat rack.

"Been shopping, have you?" Basil asked.

Marvin sniffed as he rubbed his palms together, exposing the bruises and scratches covering the top of his hands indicative of street fighting and his performances in the ring.

"Indeed, I 'ave, and it's been fantastic fun. Well, you types know about that, doncha?" He sniffed again, running the sleeve of his bathrobe under his nose. "No more scraps off the poor man's table for me." He pointed to the bottle on the table. "Can I offer you a drink?"

"No thank you, love," Ginger said.

Basil shook his head as he never took a drink while working unless the job benefitted from him doing so.

"Well, you don't mind if I help meself, do yer?" Marvin poured a shot glass, downed the contents, then flopped into a dirty armchair, breathing loudly. After a small belch, he added, "Oh, forgive my bad manners." He flicked a palm. "Do sit down. So sorry for the 'ard chairs. I plan to get everything new. *Everything* new!"

As they accepted the two kitchen chairs, Ginger noted white dust on the tabletop and shot Basil a look of alarm. Though cocaine had been banned in Britain seven years before—1920—the market had been established. If Marvin was using cocaine for pleasure, athletic enhancement, or both, he was getting it illegally, which meant he was involved with nefarious characters.

Ginger put on a disarming smile. "Marvin, we're a little worried about you."

Marvin blew hard through his lips. "I can take care of meself, madam. 'Ave me 'ole life."

Basil leaned in, resting his elbows on his knees. "I'm afraid it's a bit more serious than that. We have a witness who saw you having a row with Mr. Lester."

"Of course we were 'aving a row! You seen what 'e did, din't yer? Threw the fight! I asked 'im why. I 'ave a right to know why, don't I? Made me look like a fool, like I couldn't 'ave won that fight on me own. I could've, yer know. I could've."

Ginger frowned at Marvin's agitated state. Was he drunk, high on cocaine, or both? She worried this would become a difficult habit to break. "Marvin, perhaps you should find another line of work. Fighting is dangerous, not just because of the physicality, but because dangerous men are involved. Gangs."

Marvin pinched his eyes shut as he scoffed. Stretching a leg out to access his trouser pockets, he pulled out a wad of cash. "I 'ate being poor, Mrs. Reed. Fighting is me ticket to better times." He cocked his head. Fuelled with liquid courage that distorted his better judgement, he snidely added, "We can't all get adopted by our betters."

Basil cleared his throat. "Marvin, where did you go after your row with Lester?"

Marvin sniffed, and Basil offered his handkerchief, which Marvin accepted. After wiping his nose, he said, "I stopped at a menswear shop, went to the pubs." He chortled. "You shoulda seen their faces! Me waltzin' in with me new 'at and coat and slappin' down a bunch of coin for a bottle of their best gin. Then I came 'ere. Gin's good company."

"You don't mind if we check out your story?" Basil asked.

"What? You don't believe me?" Marvin jumped to his feet. "Do you think I'm fibbin'?"

Basil was quick to stand, holding his palms out. "Calm down. It's just routine. I need to eliminate you as a prime suspect."

Marvin's eyes, flashing with something that looked like fear, darted to Ginger. "I dint kill Lester. Why would I? I wanted a fair fight. I need to prove meself. I'd kill 'ho ever did this to 'im."

"Marvin, love," Ginger said kindly. "You mustn't speak that way, even in jest. Especially not during a murder investigation."

Marvin slumped back into his chair, defeated. "I din't kill no one, madam. You gotta believe me."

"I do," Ginger said truthfully. She didn't think Marvin had killed Lester and didn't believe him capable of such an egregious deed. At least not while sober. However, under the influence of a stimulant such as cocaine . . . well, she didn't even want to consider it. "We just want to prove it, Marvin." With a glance at the rickety bed, Ginger added, "Now, why don't you lie down and have a sleep? You'll feel better after that."

10

The next morning, Basil set out again for London's East End, this time heading for Whitechapel. Walking down the infamous dark and narrow cobblestoned street with the sound of his footsteps reverberating off the narrow, arched passage, he grimly imagined a certain foul day in 1888. Back then, the street was called George Yard. Here, the police had found the body of Martha Tabram, Jack the Ripper's first victim.

Basil often wondered if he could have brought the fiend to justice had he been working for the Yard in those days. He liked to think so.

Jimmy Willis, the corner trainer for Sid Lester, was the man Basil sought, but the address was hard to track down. When an ancient-looking black woman answered the door of the address listed in the electoral records, Basil realised the number was erroneous.

"Oh, yous lookin' for Mista Willis. Yeah, he usta live 'ere, but no more. He's not in trouble, is he?"

"No, not at all," Basil said with assurance. "I'm only looking for some information."

"Ah, well, he's got a room on Thrawl Street."

The brick building in Thrawl Street, now converted into a lodging house, looked well kept, with a black wrought-iron fence and white ornamental bricks that arched over the entrance. It was early in the day, and Basil hoped he would find Sid Lester's corner manager at home.

The landlady opened the main door and directed Basil to the correct room. When Basil knocked, the door opened almost immediately, and he recognised Jimmy Willis from the night of the fight. The man's mass of white hair, untamed by oil, and his nose, crooked from what must've been an unpleasant break —a trait Basil had realised was shared by many in the boxing world—were more shocking up close. Perhaps he'd fought as a welterweight when he was younger.

"Hello," Basil started. "I'm Chief Inspector Basil Reed from Scotland Yard. I wonder if I might have a word with you about the death of Sid Lester."

"I figured the coppers would come around soon enough," Jimmy Willis said. The dusty room had a lone bed, a couple of mismatched chairs, and a worn handwoven carpet. Old newspapers were scattered about, and Basil had to move a few pages off an armchair to clear a place to sit. A lit cigarette rested in a notch of a ceramic ashtray, its plume rising upwards.

Once they were both settled, Basil asked, "How long have you been Sid Lester's corner man?"

Willis wrinkled his crooked nose as his gaze shifted to the nicotine-stained ceiling. "Just over a year now, I guess. Yeah, I joined Lester's team in June of twenty-six." Willis reached for the cigarette in the ashtray and stuck it between his lips. "You wanna cig, sir?"

Basil shook his head. "I'm fine, thank you. Please continue."

"Righto. His previous trainer died of a heart attack. I was brought in to replace him." He exhaled a smoky breath. "I've been training boxers for years now. Used to fight myself when I was younger."

"A lot of trainers are former fighters," Basil said. "Isn't that so?"

"Uh-huh, it's a natural progression when a bloke gets too old to fight. Beats working at the docks."

"I understand you're also his manager. Did you arrange his fights for him?"

"No, that was done by several people, but mostly —" Willis broke off, tightening his lips like one did when one felt one had said too much.

"Mostly who?" Basil asked with a seriousness he hoped reminded Willis that this was a murder investigation.

After a sigh, Willis said softly, "A fellow named Sharp."

Basil jerked, but kept his composure. "I see."

"Sharp's a blighter," Willis said with a frown. "Does bad business, if you know what I mean. Now that he's out of prison, everyone's tense."

Basil wagered a guess. "He's pulling the strings?"

"Not to my face, mind," Willis said. "He's a behind-the-scenes bloke, at least most of the time."

"Who was the other man in the corner with you?" Basil asked.

"That's Colin Venables, the water boy." Willis chuckled. "Not a boy in the truest sense. He's gotta be in his forties, but that's what the job's called. He takes care of the water and other things like slapping petroleum jelly on the boxer's face or a towel for blood."

"How long has Mr. Venables been the water boy?"

"He came after me, so maybe eight months? The last water boy couldn't shake the death of the previous trainer. The nervous type. Kept saying the bloke was murdered, but the doc was clear the bloke's heart gave up. Headed back to Edinburgh last I heard. Venables is made of sterner stuff. Rubs folks up the wrong way sometimes but gets the job done."

Basil inclined his head. "What do you mean by rubbing folks up the wrong way?"

Willis lifted a shoulder. "Abrupt, rude, pushy. But that's rather standard in this business. You gotta take what's yours, or someone will snatch it from underneath yer."

"Would you consider yourself a friend of Mr. Lester?" Basil asked.

Willis shrugged. "I know he was rough around the edges, irritated folks with his brashness and conceit, but I kind of liked him. I admired his nerve. Can't believe someone shot him in cold blood like that." Willis emphasised his disbelief with a shiver.

"I have been told that Sid Lester chose to associate himself with men of questionable character," Basil said.

"I think 'chose to' is perhaps not the right way to put it."

"What do you mean?"

"Now, I keep myself distant from any kind of trouble, but I got the feeling that he resented the hold that some of these people had on him and his career."

"Like Mortimer Sharp?"

"Yes, sir."

"Do you think some of Sid Lester's fights were fixed?"

"No." Willis stubbed out his dying cigarette butt. "Not that I saw, anyway. But I do think some of his opponents were, shall we say, less than threatening for Sid. Gave him an easy win. Which is terrific for men like Sharp. He always took a big portion of Sid's winnings. Sid wasn't shy to complain to me about it. He said he felt trapped and regretted letting Mortimer Sharp manage his fights."

"Why didn't he just get a new manager?"

"I think he may have tried at some point. But..."

Basil shifted his weight as he waited. Willis' old sofa had an uncomfortable spring threatening to poke through to a sensitive area.

Willis finally continued, "I got the feeling Sharp had something on Sid."

Basil raised a dark brow. "Blackmail?"

"Could be that Sid owed him money, but Sharp was already taking whatever money he wanted, so..."

"So?" Basil prompted.

"Something kept Sid Lester under the thumb of Mortimer Sharp. Could be the powder, y'know. Seems it's everywhere and needs to come from someone, doesn't it?"

"I'm getting the feeling that drug enhancement is widespread in boxing," Basil said.

Jimmy Willis shrugged as his gaze dropped to the floor. "I really couldn't say for sure. Just an idea I had, Chief Inspector."

"What do you think happened at the last fight?" Basil leaned in. "I was there. It looked to me like Lester just gave up."

"I think he did." The corner of Willis' mouth turned down in a look of disappointment.

"I watched between rounds in your corner," Basil said. "At one point, it looked like he didn't want to hear your coaching."

"You're right about that. As the fight progressed, he got more and more irritable. A good corner man knows when to yell and when to keep quiet. Sid Lester always took my advice. But at the last fight, he was suddenly refusing to hear it. To be honest, Chief Inspector, I think he had just had enough. Only a knockout would have won the day for him, but that Marvin Elliot was just too fast."

"If that's true, if he did just give up, Sharp would've lost money."

"And money from future fights. Money to be had from betting on Sid Lester would be far less after that fight."

"Where were you when Sid Lester was shot?" Basil said.

Willis folded his arms and rocked in his chair. "I suppose that's a stock question you have to ask."

"Yes, it is."

"I was in the gym watching the exhibition match. Lots of people would have seen me."

"Did you happen to spot Marvin Elliot there?"

"Just briefly. Saw him storm out the front door. He looked angry."

The longer Basil was there, the louder the ticking clock became. With that and the uncomfortable chair, he was ready to make his departure. "Mr. Willis, do you know where I can find Colin Venables?"

"I couldn't say. But he likes to frequent The Windmill. He goes to that pub almost every day for lunch. Apparently, they serve a good steak and kidney pie."

## 11

The morning demanded Ginger's attention at home. Otherwise, she'd be making a nuisance of herself, looking for ways to nose into Basil's interviews with Sid Lester's team. The baby, however, was fretful, and Scout's tutor needed her attention. Her telephone rang seemingly incessantly—troubles with a supplier at her dress shop—and Mrs. Beasley had a complaint about the coal merchant that she couldn't cope with on her own.

All the activity caused Ginger to feel warm, and she passed her palm across a damp brow when Pippins approached.

"A young man called to see you, madam," he said, his eyes glinting in a way that Ginger guessed meant he knew the caller.

"Who is it, Pips?"

"Mr. Elliot, madam. He's waiting in the morning

room. I thought you'd like to see him." Dismay flickered across his face fleetingly. "He doesn't appear to be in a mood to be turned away quietly."

"I see." Ginger smoothed out her frock, a simple day dress with a geometric print and a large square buckle on a matching belt. She wondered what pressing circumstance would drive Marvin Elliot to come to her home and couldn't help feeling grateful that Scout was busy in the stables with Clement.

Taking a breath, Ginger stepped into the morning room. Marvin stood, holding his flat cap in his hands.

"Hello, Marvin," she said. "This is a surprise."

Marvin glanced about sheepishly. "'Ello, madam. I'm sorry to intrude."

Ginger motioned for Martin to sit and took an empty chair. She leaned in slightly, keeping her eyes on her guest. "Is there something wrong? What brings you calling?"

Marvin's knee jumped as his fingertips drummed on the arm of his chair. "It's, well, I've got a problem, madam." He stilled and squinted at her. "You're a lady detective, right? You can 'elp blokes like me?"

"It all depends on the sort of problem," Ginger said. "Why don't you tell me your problem, and I'll let you know if I can help."

The fidgeting started again. "I don't like coppers. Me and coppers don't mix."

"Is your problem a matter for the police? You know I'm not the police."

Marvin froze again. "I can't go to no coppers, madam."

"Let's back up, shall we?" Ginger said. "What is troubling you, Marvin? Clearly, something is upsetting you."

"London's a dark place, madam. Not just at night. Gangs, drugs. Forgive me for sayin' words delicate to a lady's ears."

"It's quite all right," Ginger returned. "I'm not so fragile. I'm aware of the city's drugs, gangs, and other nefarious activities."

"I don't know what nefar— what that means, but —" He lowered his voice. "I think it got Lester killed." His eyes glassed over with fear. "And I could be next."

"Why do you think that?"

"They want to own me, and if I don't let 'em—" Marvin ran a finger dramatically across his neck.

"Who wants to own you, Marvin?"

"A street gang in the East End. They offered me fifty quid. I like money as much as the next bloke, but once you take it, you—well, you become Sid Lester."

Ginger cocked her head in question. "What do you mean by that? Did this East-End gang own Mr. Lester?"

"Not them, no. He was got by The Griffin."

Ginger slumped at the mention of Mortimer Sharp's moniker and that of his group. Her own terror threatened to surface.

"Are you saying Mr. Lester was killed by, er, The Griffin?"

Marvin nodded vigorously. "What these gangs do is choose an up-'n'-comer then send 'im rubbish to fight to keep 'im the champ. That's what they did to Sid. 'E was nuffink but a puppet. I want to be legit. If I take money from the East Enders, they'll make me fight rubbish. But if I don't—"

"I understand your dilemma," Ginger said. "But I'm not sure what you want me to do for you. This is a matter for the police."

"Like I said, I don't trust coppers. I don't speak to coppers. I can't be *seen* talkin' to coppers."

"Ah," Ginger said, understanding. Marvin wanted her to look into his problem instead of Basil and the Metropolitan police. "I see. Well, I can't promise you anything, but I'll do what I can."

"That's all I ask, madam." Marvin jumped to his feet. "Scout wouldn't be around for a quick 'ello, would 'e?"

"I think he's in the back garden, in the stables." Ginger pointed through the morning-room windows to the stable buildings in the rear of the garden. "You'd be welcome to visit him there."

"Thank you, madam," Marvin said with a nod.

Ginger watched as Marvin jogged across the lawn and disappeared into the stables.

Finding Pippins, she asked him to inform Clement he was to watch over Scout and Marvin in the back garden. She checked in on Rosa, thankful to find the baby soundly asleep and a tired nanny napping in the rocking chair beside her. The view from the nursery window looked over the back garden with a clear view of the stables. Ginger watched with interest as Scout and Marvin chatted together. Marvin was smoking, but Ginger was glad to see he didn't offer his younger cousin a cigarette. After a few minutes, Marvin rubbed Scout's blond head, then disappeared into the back alley. Clement happened to glance her way, and Ginger offered a wave of thanks.

She mentally reviewed the conversation she'd had with Marvin. She found it interesting that he never mentioned his own relationship with drugs. Perhaps he was trying to kick the habit. Though, from what she'd read and from her experience with soldiers who'd become bound to drugs like cocaine and heroin in the war, it would be a hard fight, harder than anything Marvin would face in the ring.

Her mind produced an image of Marvin in the ring fighting against Sid Lester, each with men in their corner. Two for Mr. Lester and one for Marvin.

What was his corner man called again? Right, Wiley Shaftoe. The man was bound to know something. He was the most logical starting point if Ginger hoped to do what Marvin had asked.

Dressed in an ivory taffeta summer coat and matching hat, she was intercepted by Pippins at the bottom of the staircase in the entranceway.

"The afternoon post, madam," he said. "You have correspondence from France."

Ginger looked at the return address, and her breath hitched when she recognised the familiar handwriting. Sure enough, there was the name: *H. Higgins*.

## 12

The Windmill pub was old, with a low ceiling made even lower by the large wooden support beams that crossed overhead. Basil almost had to stoop to walk to keep from hitting his head.

In the corner, a fire crackled in a large stone fireplace, filling the place with the smell of hot coal. Basil scanned the room for Colin Venables, but there was no sign of the man. He ordered steak and kidney pie on Jimmy Willis' recommendation, along with a pint, and carried it to an empty table, where he settled in to wait.

His meal arrived soon afterwards, and there was still no sign of Venables. Just as Basil resigned himself to having a quiet lunch on his own, the front door opened, and two men walked in.

One man seemed familiar; the other was Mortimer Sharp

Blast! Rotten timing. Basil would've rather they'd come after he'd eaten as the sight of Sharp made him lose his appetite.

Upon seeing Basil, Sharp's hooded eyes registered no surprise or alarm but instead, a firm, steady gaze.

Basil was sure his own expression was not as inscrutable.

"Fancy meeting you here, Chief Inspector," Sharp said as he approached Basil's table.

Basil lifted his chin. "Likewise."

"I see you ordered the steak and kidney pie," Sharp said. "Good choice."

"How good of you to approve." Basil's gaze moved to the man who hovered behind The Griffin.

"Forgive my poor manners," Sharp said, his voice patronising. "This is Billy Kenmore. He works for me."

Basil recognised the henchman from the night of the fight. The well-dressed man with overly broad shoulders and a loud raspy voice was the lone person in his section shouting for Marvin to win, an oddity Basil now found even more perplexing.

"Mr. Kenmore," Basil said, motioning to the empty seats at his table. "Would you like to join me?"

Sharp's lips pulled up tightly, his smile birdlike, in the shape of a $V$ rather than a $U$.

"Nice of you to offer, Chief Inspector, but we wouldn't want to interfere with your dining pleasure."

Basil scoffed. "I'm afraid it's too late for that."

"Very well."

Sharp told Kenmore to go to the bar to order drinks and a couple of pies, then took the chair directly opposite Basil.

"The Chief Inspector and I go way back," Mortimer Sharp explained to Billy Kenmore when he returned with two pints.

"Oh really?" Kenmore's tone suggested he found the idea intriguing.

The Griffin cocked his head as he stared at Basil. "Isn't that right?"

"Unfortunately," Basil said, taking a sip of his ale. After setting it down again, he said, "How was prison life?"

"Ah, you know." Sharp waved claw-like fingers into the air. "It didn't really appeal to me."

"Wait!" Kenmore said. "Is 'e the copper that put you away?"

"The one and the same, Billy boy."

Sharp smiled at Basil as if he were some long-lost brother. "But that was a long time ago, of course. I barely remember it."

"Ha!" Billy Kenmore chortled. "That's funny 'cause I know you to be a man with great power of recall." Both chuckled at the henchman's lame attempt at humour.

Basil locked his gaze on Sharp's beady eyes. "Where were you when Sid Lester was shot?"

A man carried over two pies for Sharp and Kenmore. "Here you go, Mr. Sharp."

"See?" Sharp said, waving the man away. "*That's* respect. I didn't find your question respectful, Chief Inspector."

"Standard police procedure," Basil returned coolly. "Lester was murdered. He was your prize fighter. You had him in your pocket, and when he quit that fight early, he showed you that he was through being played for a fool. Perhaps you . . ." Basil shot Kenmore a look. "Or perhaps both of you waited at the end of the alley in your motorcar. You must have known Sid Lester was in there to collect his money. Perhaps you even sent him in there and told him you would wait outside for him. But you had already decided to send a message to all the other fighters you 'own' who might one day decide to defy you."

The two men stared at Basil with fury-filled eyes, and Basil was glad he was in a public place. "What percentage were you taking from Sid Lester? I've heard that a boxing manager makes twenty percent. What were you taking? Fifty? Sixty? More?"

Sharp's lips pulled down as he shrugged a shoulder. "I dunno. My bookkeeper takes care of that."

One of many barefaced lies, Basil imagined. Emboldened, he pushed further. "I know you're a man who doesn't like to be crossed. Isn't that true, Sharp? You like to maintain tight control, don't you? And I suspect you'll stop at nothing to ensure that control over others. You must've had something on Sid Lester that kept him subservient to you. I will find it out. I promise you."

Sharp snorted. "You think you're pretty bright, don't you?"

"I have my moments."

"And I have mine."

"Is that a threat, Sharp?"

Sharp and Kenmore cut into their meals and took a bite, Sharp chewing slowly while Kenmore wolfed his down.

"When you've finished chewing," Basil started, "perhaps you could answer my question. Where were you when Sid Lester was shot? Keep in mind you're talking to the police."

"Since you asked so nicely," Sharp said, "I was playing cards with friends. Three-card brag."

"And I suppose you have willing and well-compensated witnesses who'd confirm that," Basil said.

"Of course I have witnesses." Sharp feigned offence.

Basil stared at the henchman, who folded thick arms. "I was at the exhibition fight," Kenmore said. "Lots of blokes saw me there."

"I have to say, Chief Inspector," Sharp said with a note of playfulness. "I'm shocked at your willingness to jump to such wild conclusions about us. Sid Lester was a dear friend; no one is sadder to hear about his demise than we are. In fact, I plan to pay for his funeral. It will be a grand affair worthy of such a fine athlete."

Basil snorted. "You're terribly thoughtful."

"Thank you. Speaking of being full of thoughts, how is your lovely wife? I met her, you know, at the fight. Such a beautiful lady!"

Basil's heart skipped a beat, and he swallowed dryly. He hadn't wanted his family to be part of the discussion. Sharp, in his wily manner, had inserted his earlier veiled threat. He didn't stop there.

"And the rest of your family?" he asked. "Your adopted son and baby daughter?"

Basil tensed, his body flooding with heat. He wanted to dive across the table and grab Sharp by the scruff of his neck. He waited until the muscle in his jaw stopped twitching, then said, "I'm warning you, Sharp. You stay away from my family, or by God, I will make it my life's work to see you hang!"

As if mirroring the rage that Basil felt, in that silent moment, a piece of coal in the fireplace made a loud pop and a hiss while the flames flared.

A small, mocking smile slowly spread across Mortimer Sharp's face.

"We'll see, Chief Inspector, we'll see. Now, if you'll control yourself and resist making a scene, perhaps we can eat our pies like gentlemen."

Basil grabbed his hat and strolled out, leaving his unfinished pie and his enemy behind.

## 13

*Dear Ginger,*

*You'll be surprised and hopefully pleased that I'm in Europe! It was rather unexpected, as I thought I would complete my medical training in Boston, but a practicum in forensics opened up in Paris, and I was offered the position.*

Ginger smiled. Of course her friend would be offered the spot. Haley was highly gifted in the forensic arts, and Ginger had no doubt she placed at the top of her class. And how thrilling to know Haley was so close by!

*I arrived a week ago and only now feel like I'm no longer rocking about on the high seas. If it weren't for my deep desire to learn and hopefully see you again, I wouldn't have stepped on that rotten vessel. The Atlantic was displeased during this journey, but I'm happy to say I didn't require a bucket or the opportunity to feed the fish.*

Ginger felt giddy as she chuckled. She could hear Haley's American accent and dry-wit delivery as she read.

*If you find yourself in Paris, you must see me. I'm staying in a flat near the outskirts of the city. And, if I might be so bold, I'd be happy to cross the Channel to visit you when I have a break. The only break I know for sure is over Christmas, but I don't want to be presumptuous.*

"Presume away, my dear friend!"
"Madam?"
Ginger jerked to see Pippins watching. "It's Miss Higgins, Pips! She's on the Continent and shall be joining us for Christmas!"
"How delightful, madam."
"Christmas is so far away," Ginger said with a huff. "I must plan another trip to Paris for the shop this autumn." Short trips to Paris weren't uncommon, but Ginger hadn't made the journey since Rosa was born.

Tucking the letter into her handbag, Ginger decided she'd write back later that evening when she had more time and a clear head. Right now, she wanted to speak to Mr. Shaftoe.

The sound of Boss' nails on the marble reminded Ginger that she had recently spent little time with her pet. "Bossy, would you like to go for a motorcar ride?"

Boss' stubby black tail shimmied as he circled with eager enthusiasm.

"Come along, then."

With Boss on her heels, Ginger headed out the back entrance to the garage.

"Clement," she said to her gardener. "I'm taking the Crossley."

"Might I remove it from the garage for you, madam?" he asked eagerly. Perhaps a bit too eagerly, Ginger thought. She'd been known to hit the garage door occasionally—a simple error—and besides a few minor scratches, both the door and the motorcar were unhurt. Yet sometimes, Clement and Basil acted as if she might knock down the stone-and-mortar garage.

"Certainly." Ginger handed over the key and watched Clement smoothly move the machine. It was a handsome vehicle with a pearly-white body, white spoked tyres, and a shiny white bumper. The black hood was down, as it was for most of the summer, and the buttery-soft red leather seats were brightly polished.

Ignoring her gardener's rather choked look, she took the key. "In you go, Bossy."

Boss hopped in, taking his position on the

passenger seat on the left. The gears ground a tad unpleasantly as she found first then motored into the lane. Once there, she revved the engine, speeding along, the dust flying up behind her.

The cacophony of London always gave Ginger a certain thrill: the busy pedestrians strolling the pavements and darting amongst the motorised and non-motorised machines puttering along the road; the neighing of horses and barking of dogs—Boss' contribution included—and the honking of horns and ringing of bells. Frustrated and hurried drivers lifted fists in protest, some even directed at Ginger, which she found hilarious. She simply waved back in return.

Eventually, she found herself in front of the building where Wiley Shaftoe lived. Thanks to Marvin, she had the address.

Clipping a leash to Boss' collar, Ginger swooped him into her arms and headed for the main door. Boss was more than elbow decor—he was a bright little spark who often helped with searches and stakeouts and did his part to warn and protect her.

Ginger knew Mr. Shaftoe was a black man, so she wasn't surprised to see black children playing in the street or black mothers pushing prams. They gawked at her with suspicion, and Ginger gathered they didn't see a lot of ladies like her with such a nice car and fashionable clothing. Ginger regretted her choices for a moment, but there was nothing she could do about it now except smile.

"Hello," she said brightly.

A small group of women opened ranks and stared back at her. "I'm looking for Mr. Shaftoe. I'm here in Mr. Elliot's interest."

It was evident by the way the shoulders of the women relaxed when they heard Marvin's name that Mr. Shaftoe's means of earning a living was well known.

"Room nine," one of them said.

Ginger thanked the woman, the group closed again, and the talk resumed.

Mr. Shaftoe promptly answered the door of room nine, his dark eyes squinting in confusion. "Madam?"

"Good afternoon, Mr. Shaftoe. You don't know me, but I'm Mrs. Reed, a friend of Marvin Elliot's. He asked me to speak with you."

That wasn't precisely true, but the request was indeed insinuated.

The man's eyes landed on Boss. Ginger quickly responded, "This is Boss. He's quite friendly and will stay on my lap the whole time."

Mr. Shaftoe hesitated as if he hoped to come up with another believable and acceptable excuse to turn her away but failed. He let out a sigh. "Do come in."

Inside, the flat was simple yet tidy, with the scent of cleaner in the air.

"Would you like tea?" he asked. "I'm a widower, so I'll have to make it myself."

"I've had my fill of tea today," Ginger said with a

smile. "I shan't take up much of your time. I just have a few questions."

Mr. Shaftoe settled into a well-worn chair as Ginger balanced on the edge of the sofa, sitting on the side that sagged the least. Boss calmly lay on her lap, his pink tongue hanging out.

"So, madam, how can I help Mr. Elliot?"

"Due to the murder of Mr. Lester, Marvin is concerned for his own safety," Ginger said. "I've tried to reassure him that Mr. Lester's death was probably an isolated affair and that one fighter's demise doesn't necessarily lend itself to the next. However, that didn't seem to pacify him."

Mr. Shaftoe pushed out his lips. "There's more to fighting in the ring than meets the eye, madam. Some don't always play fair."

"You're referring to drug-taking that might help a fighter do better in the ring?"

With a nod, Mr. Shaftoe said, "Uh-huh."

"Was Mr. Lester involved in this practice?"

"I can't say."

Ginger wondered if the man couldn't say or *wouldn't* say.

"Marvin's a champ now; that's the main thing."

"He is," Ginger said, "but he's not very happy about it. He wants to prove that he could win without his opponent quitting mid-fight."

"And he will, madam. Young Elliot's got *fire* in his belly."

## MURDER AT THE BOXING CLUB

Ginger believed that too, only she was afraid that Marvin's fire didn't originate from his belly but from illegal white powder.

"Mr. Shaftoe, do you have any reason to believe that Marvin has ever taken drugs? Sniffed cocaine?"

Folding his arms, Mr. Shaftoe snorted. "Not in my presence."

"That's not really an answer."

Mr. Shaftoe pushed against the arms of his chair and rose to his feet. Boss squirmed, emitting a low growl.

Ginger whispered in his ear. "It's all right, Bossy. We're going now."

Ginger noted that Mr. Shaftoe was no taller than she was, though, by the strength of his physique, he clearly knew more about boxing than what came from a book or observation

"Thank you for your time," she said, rising from the chair. "Just one more question. Does the club manager know his fighters take drugs?"

Mr. Shaftoe chuckled. "That would be a question for Mr. Friar, but I wouldn't expect a straight answer, madam."

"Are you saying he'll lie?"

The glint of humour left Mr. Shaftoe's brown eyes. "I didn't say it, madam. You did."

14

"I originally looked for you at the Windmill pub," Basil said as he approached a table at the Regency Eatery occupied by Colin Venables. A slight-looking man in his mid-forties, Venables wore thick black-framed glasses, which he often pushed up on his nose. So far, he was the only man Basil had encountered on this investigation who didn't look like he had spent time in the ring. Besides his lack of physique, his nose was perfectly straight. Basil would have placed him in an accountant's office or something similar.

"I heard you frequent there for lunch," Basil added.

"I often do," Venables said. "I like to have a change now and again, though. And you are?"

"Chief Inspector Basil Reed from Scotland Yard."

"Ah." Venables squirmed in his seat. "You're investigating the alley shooting."

"Indeed. Do you mind if I join you?"

It was a rhetorical question, and they both knew it.

Basil claimed an empty chair. Venables lifted a spoonful of tomato soup to eager lips, his hand quivering slightly, blowing on it before sipping it down.

"I hope you don't mind a brief interruption to your lunch," Basil continued, "but I just have a few questions."

"Don't worry, Chief Inspector." Venables used his handkerchief to swipe at his nose. "I knew I would be questioned at some point, but I haven't got all day."

"I'll be brief," Basil said. "Do you work with fighters besides Lester?"

Venables pushed up on his glasses. "I do now. Can't work with the dead, can I?"

"What is your background in boxing?"

Venables patted his lips and his nose once again. "It's the soup," he said as if needing to explain. "Makes my nose run."

Basil asked again, "About your background in boxing?"

"Yes, well, as you can probably tell," he started, his knee jiggling under the table, "I'm not the athletic type, but I was always fascinated by the sport. I've been hanging around boxing clubs for most of my life."

"Here in Bethnal Green?" Basil asked.

"No, I grew up in Yorkshire."

Basil grinned. "Aha, I thought I detected an accent."

"Hah, I guess the secret's out now," Venables said. "Are you gonna go and order?"

"No, but you carry on with your lunch."

Another sniff was followed by a slurp of soup.

"How did you come to work with the Sid Lester team then?" Basil asked.

"Friar hired me."

"Friar and not Lester?"

"They're one and the same. Friar does what he's told, and Lester did what he was told. Monkeys obeying their music man."

Basil rubbed his chin thoughtfully. "Who's the 'music man'?"

Venables' gaze scanned the eatery, his shoulders sinking in. With cold eyes, he said, "If I tell you that, I might end up like Lester."

"Dead?"

"I'd prefer to keep my nose clean if you know what I mean."

Basil could guess, but he'd rather hear it from Venables' lips. "I'm afraid I don't."

Venables leaned over his empty bowl, his tie nearly missing a soup washing. "It's them gangs. They own the lot. Friar, Lester . . ."

Basil reluctantly filled in the blank. "Elliot?"

Venables leaned back. "I dunno. If they don't yet, they soon will. Blasted sport's gone and got corrupted."

Basil kept his expression blank. Venables had only confirmed what he'd suspected. "How did you like working with Sid Lester?"

Venables slurped his last spoonful of soup, then said, "Working with a winner has its perks. Corner men get paid on percentage just like managers and trainers, but..."

"But?"

Venables took a swig of his beer. After a small belch, he added, "It also has its drawbacks."

"I've heard Lester was hard to get along with," Basil said. "Is that what you mean?"

"He was a surly one, all right." Venables' focus darted about the room. "Dealing with his moods was just part of the job."

Basil circled back to Venables' mention of gangs. "What do you know about The Griffin?"

Venables huffed. "Nothin' that you probably don't know."

"Humour me," Basil said. "If you know something, Venables, and withhold it from me, well, it could be seen as obstruction of justice."

Venables' eyes shifted, clearly conflicted. Then, as if coming to a decision, he leaned in and lowered his voice. "The blighter takes fifty percent of the winnin's. That's far more than a normal manager's cut. He gets more for doin' nothin'."

"Did you ever hear him threaten Sid Lester?"

Venables pushed on his spectacles. "No, not that I

remember specifically."

"One theory is that Sid Lester should've fought longer but quit when he realised he couldn't get a good swing at Marvin Elliot."

Venables scoffed. "That boy is just too fast. Sid Lester punched hard but had slow feet."

"Isn't it true that quitting that fight would rob Mr. Sharp of considerable future earnings?" Basil asked.

"Yes, both in manager's fees and sports bettin'." Venables pushed his dirty dishes to the side, then sipped his beer. "When I heard that someone had shot Sid Lester . . . well, let's just say Sharp and his stupid henchman, Kenmore, were the first names that came to mind."

"I see."

"Them, and Thomas Friar too."

"The club manager?" Basil asked. "Why him?"

"He's always hobnobbin' with Sharp and Kenmore. Like the blasted Three Musketeers."

"Interesting," Basil said. "Friar told me that he kept his distance from people like that. In fact, he said he told Sid Lester to keep them out of the club."

"Ha!" Venables snorted into his handkerchief. "That's a laugh. Friar needs them to get the drugs."

"Cocaine?"

Venables nodded. "Uh-huh. I saw white powder on Friar's desk."

"Perhaps it was talcum powder," Basil offered. "For sweaty palms."

## MURDER AT THE BOXING CLUB

With a shake of his head, Venables said, "I rubbed a bit on my gums. Immediately numb. I also saw Friar hand a small bag to a young fighter once. He looked around first like he was doing somethin' secretive. He didn't see me around the corner." He clucked his tongue and added, "Like I said, rampant."

"You should have reported that, you know?" Basil said, wondering how Colin Venables knew cocaine made one's gums numb.

"And lose my job? Ha! I'm not bigger than Mortimer Sharp, and frankly, neither are you."

Basil huffed at the man's apparent low esteem for the law but let the slight go. "Where were you when Sid Lester was killed?"

"I was at the exhibition match in the buildin' at that time."

"Were you working in it?"

"No, just watchin'. Willis was in the winner's corner."

"Jimmy Willis?" Basil asked. That would give the corner man a firm alibi.

"Yes, sir."

"Mr. Venables, do you own a gun?"

Venables frowned as he adjusted his spectacles and pushed away from the table. "No, sir."

Basil headed for the door, but he stopped short when he glanced over his shoulder. Venables was talking to a fellow in a wheelchair, and even from Basil's position at the opposite end of the restaurant, he could see the conversation wasn't amiable. Venables kicked the wheelchair and stormed out the back—as if he owned the place—instead of leaving through the front entrance like the rest of the customers.

Basil was about to turn back to question the man in the wheelchair when movement at the door caught his eye. Braxton stepped inside.

"Oh, sir, I'm so glad I've found you!" his constable said, a tad out of breath. "There's been a shooting."

Braxton wouldn't be bothering him about another unrelated murder case in the city. Basil jumped to the conclusion. "Another boxer?"

Braxton nodded soberly. "Yes, sir. It's Marvin Elliot, sir."

AN AMBULANCE and two police motorcars were parked outside Marvin's boarding house. A street constable stood outside the entrance, scrutinising people going in. Upon recognising Basil, he immediately nodded and stepped aside.

Basil's heart sank when he saw two ambulance attendants carrying a stretcher out of the front door. On it lay the unconscious and pale form of Marvin Elliot. His head was bandaged, and wisps of hair that stuck out between the folds of linen were matted with blood.

*Good Lord.*

Basil pushed back a sense of regret. Ginger had

told him that Marvin had come to see her. With everything happening so quickly, Basil just hadn't got around to seeking Marvin out.

He approached the doctor observing the ambulance attendants, his black doctor's bag in hand.

"Doctor?" Basil started. "Is he . . . ?"

"It's a miracle he's alive, Chief Inspector, and I mean that in the most literal way. Shot ran along the side of his head, and it appears the bullet cracked his skull and skimmed his brain. I've managed to staunch some of the bleeding for now, but I need to get him to the operating theatre if there's any hope of keeping him alive."

Basil stepped out of the man's way, watching until they had loaded Marvin into the ambulance. Once the vehicle disappeared around the corner, he rushed back to the flat, to where he'd already dispatched Braxton. Sergeant Scott was at the scene, his camera at the ready.

A small paper bag containing tobacco for rolling cigarettes was on the kitchen table. It appeared that Marvin had likely just returned from the tobacconist. Blood was splattered on the floor and wall.

Braxton conferred with two other younger officers. "A very brazen shooting, sir," Braxton said when he spotted Basil. "In broad daylight, around two o'clock this afternoon, in a building full of tenants. I've sent a couple of officers out to question the neighbours."

"Very good, Braxton," Basil said quietly. The scene

and the situation naturally unnerved him. "Who summoned the police?"

"The landlady who lives next door. She's already given her statement to the attending constable." Braxton pulled out a notepad, squinting as he read his own notes. "The woman said she heard a strange sound but didn't recognise it as a gunshot. More like a crash."

"Like the sound of Marvin falling to the floor," Basil said. "It's odd she didn't hear a gunshot, though, isn't it? Perhaps the weapon had been equipped with a suppressor of some kind."

"My thoughts too, sir. Anyway, she thought it'd be a good time to collect the rent Mr. Elliot owed her—he was a month late—and when he didn't answer, she tried the door, which was unlocked."

Basil studied the doorframe, finding no signs of forced entry. "Elliot may have let the killer in. Perhaps they knew each other. Or the person followed Marvin off the street, keeping his distance, and then simply walked right in soon after Marvin went into the flat." Basil waved a gloved hand. "Continue with your search, Constable. Of course, we're looking for signs of theft, though I suspect this assault wasn't due to a botched robbery."

Braxton touched his helmet. "Yes, sir."

Basil turned to Scott. "Sergeant, was Elliot found on his back?"

"He was, sir." Scott pointed to the area on the floor in front of what was clearly Marvin's favourite chair, the very one he had sat in when Basil and Ginger had recently visited. The sergeant continued. "His back was to the window."

The thickness of the blood splatter indicated a close-range shot. Basil positioned himself where he judged the shooter might have stood.

"How many shots were fired?" Basil asked.

"I found one casing, sir," Scott said. "The mashed-up bullet fragment was found in the wall by the window. It and the casing are on their way to evidence."

Basil stared at the dent in the wall by the window. "Doubtful that a mashed-up fragment will tell us much."

A careful shooter might have stopped to pick up the bullet casing after firing the shot, even though it would have cost him an extra moment. The gunman, no doubt, believed he'd accomplished his goal. Basil was determined to keep the truth of Marvin's survival from the papers as long as possible.

"Sir?" Braxton's voice caught his attention. "You might want to take a look at this."

On a small countertop around the gas ring was a spattering of white powder. Basil bent to examine it closely with Braxton's magnifying glass. He carefully wet his little finger and applied a small amount to his gums.

*Sweet.* With relief, he said, "Sugar. I'm sure you'll find a bowl of it somewhere."

"Yes, sir," Braxton said. "I've searched the whole flat, sir. No signs of robbery, although we won't know for sure until we can question Mr. Elliot about any missing items. I did find fifty quid in the chest of drawers."

"A goodly amount of money that would have been easily found by any thief worth their salt," Basil said.

"Agreed, sir."

After directing Braxton to finish at the flat and question the neighbours, Basil steered his Austin towards South Kensington.

He wasn't looking forward to breaking the news of the attempt on Marvin's life to Ginger. Telling Scout would be even harder.

## 15

The moment Ginger saw Basil's face, she knew something was wrong. She pushed herself out of her office chair as Basil took a long stride towards her.

"Please sit down," he said.

Ginger slowly lowered herself. "What's wrong, Basil?" She made a mental list of her loved ones: Rosa was with the nanny in the nursery, and Scout was reading in the library. The household staff was all accounted for. She'd just returned from Felicia's house, having stopped in for tea.

Basil sat before her.

"It's Marvin," she said.

With a sober nod, Basil confirmed her fears. "He's alive, love. I'm not sure how it's possible, but—"

"What happened?"

"He was shot in the head. It appears he'd only been back in his flat for a short time."

Ginger blinked. "Shot in the head?" She'd seen many soldiers with gunshot wounds in the war, but rarely did they live with a bullet to the head.

"It was a clean shot. The doctor said it missed the mass of his brain." Basil rubbed the back of his neck. "I'm afraid he's not out of the woods yet."

"Oh mercy." Ginger's hand went to her chest as she inhaled. "Do you know who's responsible?"

"The landlady heard Marvin fall to the floor but didn't hear a gun blast."

"The gunman must've used a suppressor," Ginger said, "which means—"

"A professional job."

Ginger felt light-headed at the implications. "Mortimer Sharp?"

"Likely a henchman," Basil replied. "He's not the type of fellow to get his hands dirty if he can help it."

"Any witnesses?" Ginger asked.

"Not so far, but the officers are canvassing."

Ginger placed a hand on her forehead. "We have to tell Scout."

"I'll do that," Basil said. "In the meantime, we must alert the family."

Ginger's chin shot up. "What do you mean? Surely this has to do with the boxing club and bad bets?"

It was Basil's turn to rub his face in his hands. "We

don't have a clear motive or proof of the gunman's identity. Perhaps the fact that Marvin is related to our son is merely a coincidence. But—"

"Perhaps not," Ginger finished weakly. "We need to tell everyone before they read it in the newspapers or hear it reported on the wireless."

"Indeed," Basil said. "Where might I find Scout?"

"He's in the library."

After Basil had left in search of Scout, Ginger sent Lizzie across the court to give a message to Burton to pass on to Felicia and Charles, inviting them for tea and receiving important information. An idea brewed in Ginger's mind, and she'd need Charles' help to pull it off. But first, she'd have to do some major convincing.

Ginger told Pippins to show the Davenport-Witts to the drawing room when they arrived and to have one of the maids bring tea. She then escorted Ambrosia down the hall.

"Where's the fire?" Ambrosia sputtered as Ginger guided her by the arm. The tapping of Ambrosia's walking stick clicked rapidly on the marble tiles."

"No fire," Ginger said, slowing down. "I've got family news that I want to tell everyone when Felicia and Charles arrive, that's all."

"Family news?" Ambrosia said. "Shouldn't that be Felicia's news?"

That Felicia was expecting wasn't widely known, not even within the family, and Ginger was rather surprised that Ambrosia had figured it out. Well, perhaps she shouldn't have been so surprised. Ambrosia had lived a long while and had nothing better to do than observe the lives of others.

"Oh," Ambrosia cast Ginger a round-eyed look. "It's not you, again? With the family news?"

"It's not anything like that, Grandmother."

The drawing room was on the opposite side of the entrance hall from the sitting room, with tall windows facing Mallowan Court. Modern furniture with jade velvet upholstery, plush vertical seams along the backs, and ornate wooden frames were arranged in front of a brick fireplace. The walls, papered in patterns of ivory and green, had painted portraits of Ginger's parents hanging in ornate frames. An underused baby grand piano took up the remaining space.

Ambrosia settled into a chair facing the fireplace, the large knuckles of her hands whitening as she leaned on her walking stick. The jewelled baubles on her fingers reflected the light from the electric lamps.

"Ginger, Grandmama," Felicia said upon entering the drawing room. She held the midsection of her shapeless frock—an unconscious giveaway—as she stepped to her grandmother, kissing her on the cheek.

"Welcome," Ginger said. "Come, Charles, have a seat."

The earl, wearing cuffed trousers and a crisply starched shirt under a woollen V-neck waistcoat, took a spot on the sofa as Felicia sat beside him.

"Ginger?" Felicia started. "Is everything all right? Your message sounded urgent."

"I'll get to that in a moment," Ginger said.

The maid, Grace, arrived with a drinks trolley which held a tray with pot of tea and carrying several crystal decanters containing spirits of varying colours ranging from purple to burned umber. Ginger smiled inwardly at what was clearly an initiative put forward by her intuitive butler.

"Charles?" she said with a nod towards the trolley.

Charles tugged on his trousers before standing. "I don't mind if I do. Anyone else?"

Ginger was about to accept a glass of sherry when Basil entered. "I was told you'd all be here."

"It's a party," Ambrosia said dryly. "If only we knew what we were celebrating."

Drinks were delivered, with Felicia having tea. The ladies sat on the sofa and chairs, and Basil and Charles moved to stand near the fireplace.

Ambrosia tapped the floor lightly with her walking stick. "I don't have youth on my side, Ginger, so I'd appreciate it if you'd get on with it. You know I hate being kept in suspense."

"Of course," Ginger said. "I'm afraid I have distressing news about Marvin Elliot. He's been shot. He's alive, thank goodness, but someone tried to kill him."

"Who would do such a thing?" Felicia asked, looking alarmed. "And why?"

Ginger shared a look with Basil, who nodded as he raised his glass of brandy to his lips. "Basil and I have an enemy," she said, "who's become a serious threat to our family."

"An enemy?" Ambrosia said. "We're not at war. We're civilised English people."

"Sometimes," Basil began, "in my line of work, one can cross a devious personality who takes the job of the police personally."

Ambrosia harrumphed. She'd never hidden having thought that Ginger's decision to marry a man engaged with the police force, even a man of means and good breeding, was beneath her former granddaughter-in-law. Though, Ginger thought the Gold family matriarch had warmed up to him over time.

"I'm assuming this has to do with the danger Elliot found himself in," Charles said. "But isn't that connected with the boxing world and the first death?"

"It might be," Ginger said. "But it might not. The man who has become our enemy is the father of the woman who tried to kill Basil in the spring, and they have both made threats against us all. Until he's apprehended, we can't be assured of our safety."

Felicia gripped the string of beads around her neck. "Do you really think we're all in danger?"

"This maniac might go after one of you, or worse, one of the children, just to get back at me," Basil said. "I'm very sorry to have put you in this situation."

"It's not your fault, love," Ginger said.

"What is it that you propose we do?" Ambrosia said. "Are we all to arm ourselves now? Employ men to follow us about?"

"You think we need to leave London, don't you?" Felicia said. "I suppose we could go back to Bray Manor. It's not all been burned down."

Ginger didn't think even the quiet English countryside would be safe enough from the likes of Mortimer Sharp. "Actually, I propose that you leave the country."

Ambrosia blustered again. "You want us to leave the country? And where do you propose we go?"

"France," Ginger said. "We could rent a villa there." She didn't feel her good news about Haley Higgins being in Paris and her own happiness at the prospect of seeing her again was appropriate to bring up at this moment.

"Capital idea," Basil said. He shot Ginger a look of admiration. "Think of it as a French holiday!"

"All of us?" Felicia glanced at her husband. "Charles? You'd come too?"

Basil reached over to Charles and patted his shoulder. "If he would do so, I would be indebted, as I will need to stay behind to help bring this scoundrel to justice. My good man, would you take the lead and escort the ladies and children to safety?"

Charles' eyes flashed with dark worry. "Of course. When should we leave?"

"Sooner is better than later," Ginger said. She

wouldn't rest easy until her loved ones on English soil were far away from Mortimer Sharp and anyone connected with him.

16

After their impromptu family meeting had dispersed, Ginger took Basil's arm. "How did Scout take the news?"

"Not well, but he's comforted that Marvin is still alive. At least—" Basil flashed Ginger a worried look. "I hope he is."

"Is Scout still with Mr. Fulton?" Ginger asked. She didn't want Scout to be alone when he heard the news.

"Yes. I asked the fellow to stay with him a bit longer today."

"Good idea," Ginger said.

Basil checked his wristwatch. "I'm going to check on Marvin at the hospital."

"I'm coming too," Ginger said.

"I don't—"

Ginger held a finger to her husband's lips. "He's family. He was afraid of something or someone, and now we know he had a right to be. I simply must see him for myself."

She steadied a wide-eyed look on Basil, one that warned him not to try to deny her, and after a short stand-off, Basil relented.

"Very well," he said. "It's unlikely we'll encounter any real danger at the hospital. Competent officers are guarding his room."

Ginger read the doubt in Basil's eyes. It would be a rare copper who could stand up to the likes of The Griffin.

"I'll be fine," she said reassuringly. "I have you to protect me." And her small Remington derringer pistol she carried in her handbag.

The drive north to the Royal Free Hospital was quieter than usual, with Basil at the wheel of his Austin. He seemed to focus his attention on the busy and rather chaotic streets. Ginger, however, allowed her mind to drift as the familiar area of Belsize Park passed by. How had they got to this place, fearing for her family to the degree she'd want them to leave England? Was Marvin's attack related to Sid Lester's death? Was it a signal to those involved in drugs and sports betting?

Or was it personal?

She faced Basil, speaking loudly, "Have any witnesses come forward yet?"

"Braxton interviewed two people who say they saw an unfamiliar man leaving the building just after the shooting would have happened. Neither heard any shots. They both say the man was elderly, in his late sixties or more, wearing a flat cap and walking with the use of a cane."

"A disguise," Ginger said.

"I think so, yes. It supports the bloke's brazen attitude. He knew we wouldn't be able to find him once he left the building." Basil gripped the steering wheel while guiding the motorcar around a slow-moving horse and cart. "This case is dashed complicated. We have a champion boxer with known ties to criminal elements who was shot in an alley by someone apparently waiting for him in a motorcar. So far, there are no witnesses to the shooting except a beat constable who heard the shots and the screeching of tyres. Fresh tyre marks at the end of the alley pointed east down Old Ford Road where there are fewer witnesses and intersections."

"Meaning the killer knew the area," Ginger added. "Or killers. There could've been a driver and a gunman."

"Exactly," Basil said with a short nod. "The suspected motive is retribution. He was to be made an example of. The victim went against the rules by throwing a fight, ending a considerable income stream for the criminals who controlled him."

"Who are the main suspects?" Ginger asked.

"Our friend Mortimer Sharp, of course, since he was apparently Sid Lester's manager and the one with the most to lose." Basil stopped at a crossroads, looked right, then left before continuing.

"Or his employee, Billy Kenmore," Ginger said.

"Witnesses place him at the exhibition fight underway at the time."

"But he could have slipped out unnoticed."

Basil concurred. "Indeed. In fact, when I interviewed Colin Venables—"

"Sid Lester's water boy—"

"Yes. He pointed to Kenmore."

"They all accuse one another," Ginger said. "Don't they?"

Reaching the hospital, Ginger and Basil stopped at the nurses' desk. Basil identified himself, and they were given Marvin's room number.

An officer stood to attention outside his door. "Hello, sir," he said when he saw them. "Madam."

Basil had arranged for Marvin to have a private room rather than be out on the ward with the other patients. The room was dimly lit and sparsely furnished with only a white metal-framed bed, a single mattress, and a bedside table. A white curtain hung at a lone window.

Marvin lay still under the white blanket, his head heavily wrapped in gauze and his skin pale and pasty, a profound change from the vibrant young man Ginger knew. She had to hold in a gasp, finding herself fixated on his chest's slow rise and fall.

Approaching the bed, Ginger took Marvin's limp hand in hers.

"Marvin?" she said gently. "It's Mrs. Reed. You're not alone."

Ginger swallowed her disappointment. She'd hoped the sound of her voice, the presence of someone who cared about him, would rouse him from his catatonic state. It would bring so much relief if he'd regain consciousness. She thought of Scout and how important Marvin was to him. And, of course, he might be able to reveal his attacker.

"He looks so . . . vulnerable," she said.

Despite Ginger's best hope, Marvin didn't rouse. She and Basil sat in the empty visitors' chairs, watching him. Who'd done this to Marvin? Was his attack related to the Lester murder?

Ginger leaned towards Basil and whispered, "What about Sid Lester's trainer?"

"Jimmy Willis," Basil whispered back. "His alibi is solid. He was the corner trainer of one of the fighters at the exhibition. Multiple witnesses saw him there at the precise time the murder occurred."

Ginger's mind raced as she watched the rise and fall of Marvin's chest. The people most closely connected with Sid Lester seemed to have been in the crowd at that fight. Any one of them, except for Jimmy Willis, could have slipped out of the building unnoticed.

A doctor entered, wearing the standard white lab

coat complemented with a stethoscope hung around his neck and a clipboard in his hand. Ginger and Basil rose to their feet.

"Are you family?" he asked.

Simultaneously Ginger said, "Yes," while Basil said, "Police."

Basil explained, "It's both. I'm Chief Inspector Basil Reed, and this is my wife, Mrs. Reed. Mr. Elliot is related to our adopted son."

"I see," the doctor said. "Mr. Elliot is a lucky man, indeed. We don't often see survivors of brain injuries such as this. In fact, he's created quite a stir amongst the medical fraternity in this city."

"Will there be any permanent damage?" Ginger asked. It was the question she dreaded posing, and she held her breath while waiting for the answer.

"We won't know until he regains consciousness," the doctor said. "*If* he regains consciousness. Despite his good fortune, his injury is extremely serious. I would prepare for the worst, Mrs. Reed, I'm sorry to say."

When the doctor left, Ginger put her hand on Marvin's arm and spoke softly in his ear. "Mr. Reed and I are here for you. Scout is waiting for you too. We are all cheering you on, Marvin. You are a fighter; now fight! Nothing else matters right now."

## 17

Upon leaving the hospital, Ginger and Basil agreed that returning to the first crime scene was in order. One's mind worked differently on a second pass—the ability to think on a level beyond the means of death, circumstantial evidence, and primary witnesses to the smaller details of motive, movement, and missed clues.

Ginger glanced at Basil, who tightly gripped the steering with gloved hands. The tension was evident in the stiffness of her husband's shoulders and the tightness of his jaw. Ginger felt stiff with anxiety as well, particularly for Marvin. "Are you sure he's safe?"

"Marvin?" Basil returned. "Of course. There's no safer place."

"Do you think he knew his attacker?" Ginger asked.

"It's difficult to say for sure," Basil said. "But I

suspect his attacker waited outside and simply followed him in."

"He was facing the gunman when the gun went off," Ginger stated.

"Perhaps Marvin failed to close the door completely. In any case, the gunman just walked in. The interior walls of that building aren't well made. That no one heard the shot means it was quite likely that a sound suppressor was used."

"He must've been in a hurry to leave," Ginger said. "He didn't even check to see if Marvin was dead, though head wounds produce a lot of blood. The gunman likely thought the deed was done."

"Very brazen. Done in broad daylight, like that."

She and Basil shared a look. Mortimer's daughter had proven to be a master of disguise, and possibly the skill ran in the family.

"Word has probably got out that Marvin is still alive," Ginger said pensively. "They will try to come after him."

"No need to worry, love." Basil reached over to squeeze her hand. "He's well guarded."

Ginger's mind wandered as Basil's Austin continued to rumble along. She'd tasked her family to prepare for a stay in France, but she had done nothing to prepare. Lizzie would help pack her wardrobe, certainly, as she was well versed in which frocks and gowns Ginger preferred and the necessary shoes, hats, and jewellery needed to go with them. But there was the matter of her businesses, Feathers & Flair and Lady Gold Investigations. She needed to advise Madame Roux of the changes.

Ginger was pulled out of her reverie by Basil's voice. "That's where I interviewed Venables."

"Where?"

"That restaurant with the blue-copper overhang. The Regency Eatery."

Ginger noted the establishment, part of a row of businesses in a connected brick-and-stone structure.

"Is that a ramp?" Ginger said, eyeing the wooden plank that met the door from the opposite side of the steps.

"Braxton mentioned that a man in a wheelchair, a former soldier, owns the place."

Ginger nodded in approval. "Good for him."

They reached the corner of Old Ford Road and the alley behind the boxing club, and Basil brought the Austin to a stop. The alley was enclosed with a brick wall running parallel to the building and then perpendicular, creating a dead end where the rubbish bins were stored. A public park existed on the other side of the wall, which was too tall to see over.

"We haven't turned up a single new witness," Basil said with a note of frustration in his voice. "This brick wall keeps the boxing club business from flowing onto the park behind it."

"With the nefarious goings-on behind the club,"

Ginger started, "the barrier adds protection to random pedestrians and riders in the park."

"I released a statement in the papers asking anyone who might've seen something to report it to the police on the chance someone driving by might've spotted the getaway motorcar, but so far, nothing."

Ginger's gaze landed on the two vehicles parked near the boxing club door, across from the rubbish bins. She pointed to the end of the alley, blocked off from whatever lay behind it by the continuation of the brick wall. "Is that where the motorcar was parked?" she asked. "The one driven by the killer?"

"According to the beat cop on duty, yes."

As Ginger and Basil walked the lane to the wall, she tried to picture the scene in her mind. The killer must've been waiting for the right moment, knowing that Mr. Lester was inside the club picking up his pay and would depart at any time.

"How had the killer known that Sid Lester would be alone in the alley?" she said.

Basil lifted a shoulder. "Perhaps the killer didn't care. If this was a gang setup, well, they have little or no consideration for collateral damage."

They were about to walk back towards Basil's motorcar when Ginger caught sight of rusted iron sticking through a knot of vines. As she got closer, she saw an outline of a door.

"Basil?"

"Yes, love."

"It's a door handle." Ginger gave the handle a shake, but it was stiff and not easily moved.

"By Jove, I think you're right," Basil said. "Let me give it a go."

Basil put his strength into it, and the handle disengaged. The door inched open with a shove of his shoulder.

"It only gives about twelve inches," Basil said. "Something is blocking it from the other side." He poked his head and shoulders around to look. "A tree has grown in the way."

"The opening is large enough for someone to slip into or out of the alley," Ginger said.

"Perhaps," Basil concurred, "but it would be tough for a big fellow to get through."

Basil stepped back to allow Ginger to look. The door opened just wide enough for her to slip through. Was it possible that a woman had killed Sid Lester? Were they completely on the wrong track?

Beyond the wall was a patch of the park extending along the back of the row of buildings that included the Regency Eatery. A small patio was situated behind the restaurant, where a man sat in a wheelchair. He spotted Ginger staring his way, and his eyes narrowed to an unfriendly glare.

Basil watched from the door. "What's that?"

"The man in the wheelchair seems unhappy," Ginger said, stepping back into the alley. "Did you meet him when you spoke to Colin Venables?"

Basil shook his head as he closed the door, ensuring the vines weren't in the way. "I never had the pleasure. But I did witness a rather unpleasant exchange between him and Venables."

"Is that so?" Ginger said with growing curiosity.

They walked back down the alley and beyond the wall to the park's edge. An older man in green overalls and a flat cap pushed a wooden wheelbarrow to a bed of flowers.

On a whim, Ginger approached the man. "Good day, sir," she said cheerily.

Without acknowledging Ginger's presence, the man knelt slowly, as if his joints needed a good oiling, and plucked weeds.

Basil, joining Ginger, cleared his throat and spoke a little louder, "Good day to you, sir."

"What?" Surprised, the man looked up at Ginger and Basil and, with a slow effort, rose to his feet again.

"I said, good day, sir," Basil repeated. "We're sorry to startle you."

The man's grey brows formed a deep *V* as his focus darted between Ginger, Basil, and the street as if he were wondering how the devil they had appeared out of nowhere to disturb his important work.

"I'm Chief Inspector Basil Reed from Scotland Yard," Basil said. "And this is my wife, Mrs. Reed."

"Scotland Yard, you say?" The man spoke loudly like one does when one suffers from a hearing impairment.

"Yes, that's right," Basil said. "Would you mind if we ask you a few questions?"

"You'll have to speak up, sir." The man pointed to his ears, then waved. "I can't hear a blasted word you're saying unless you speak up. Scotland Yard or not."

Basil raised his voice to just under a shout, "I wonder if I might ask you some questions, sir?"

"That's much better, Inspector, but I don't know what you might want to ask me."

"I take it you're the groundskeeper here for this park?"

"Yes, sir."

"By any chance, were you working here two days ago in the afternoon?" Ginger asked loudly.

The man's eyes grew wider. "Don't tell me that dashed idiot ran someone over!"

"Sorry. What do you mean?" Basil said.

"That idiot that almost ran me off me bike." The man pointed across the street to the boxing club.

"Someone was driving recklessly?" Ginger asked.

"He certainly was. I was just leaving here. I ride me bicycle to get across the gardens. Some bloke came tearing out of that alleyway there and almost hit me straight on. I had to swerve mightily, or I would've been knocked flying."

"You didn't hear a gunshot before he rounded the corner?"

"A gunshot? No, I didn't. Did someone get shot too?" The man's eyes went wide as saucers.

"Yes, there was a murder committed right in that alley," Basil said. "You haven't read about it in the papers?"

"No, I don't read the papers much. Not since me wife died two years ago, God rest her soul. Too much bad news in the world, and me poor soul can't take it. I stick to me job and keep my head down."

"We understand," Ginger shouted kindly. "You're saying this motorcar nearly hit you?"

"That's right. I dusted meself off and kept riding home. I was shaking like a leaf."

Which would explain why the canvassing officers missed speaking to him, Ginger mused.

"So, to be clear," Basil said, "this would have happened around what time?"

The man cupped his ear. "Huh?"

Basil shouted. "At what time?"

"I leave here the same time every day after I put the garden tools back in the main shed over there." He pointed to a wooden shed under a grove of trees just across the small grassy meadow. "Then I head over to Lansdowne Park."

"At what time?" Basil repeated, making sure his voice was loud enough.

"Three o'clock."

Ginger glanced at Basil. That was when the shooting was thought to have happened.

"Did you get a good look at the driver?" Ginger asked.

"Not really. His head was turned around. That's why he didn't see me, I s'pose. Damn fool. It all happened too fast anyway. I was lying on the pavement by the time he went past me."

Basil stepped closer to the man. "I don't suppose you remember what kind of motorcar it was?"

"I certainly do. I made sure I got a look at it before it went out of my sight. It was a blue 1924 Daimler D16 Landaulette." The gardener grinned. "The kind where you can fold down the rear part of the roof."

Basil's eyebrows shot up. "It's impressive that you know the exact model."

"Me grandson is a motorcar mechanic. He talks about nothing else. I can do better than that, though." The man shook his finger in the air. "Me ears might be too dull to have heard the shot, but my eyes are still good. And I pride meself on keeping me wits about me too."

He reached into the breast pocket of his overalls and pulled out a small piece of paper.

"I meant to contact the police about this, but I haven't had a chance yet."

He held the note out to Basil, who read it, then handed it to Ginger with a crooked grin on his face.

The note had AL 6795 scribbled in pencil. The man had just given Basil the registration number of the getaway car.

## 18

"Do you want to go inside to call in the registration number?" Ginger asked.

Basil frowned. "The boxing club doesn't have a telephone. I believe it's vital we track the number as soon as possible. The police station isn't far from here. Let's call there and then come back."

"Why don't I wait for you here," she said. "I can snoop around a bit."

Basil's frown deepened. "The establishment is filled with men, Ginger. It could be precarious."

Ginger inclined her head, giving her husband a kind but firm look. "I'll be fine. It's not like anyone is going to attack me in public. Besides, putting a fellow off balance can be an effective strategy."

"Ginger—"

"Basil, I'll be fine. Surely you must know that by now." She waved a hand. "I'll wait here in the lobby."

Basil looked as if he was about to bare his teeth and growl his dissent but then wisely stepped back. "Very well. I'll be as speedy as I can. Do try to stay out of trouble, Ginger."

Ginger smirked in return. "I'll do my best, love."

Basil shot her a look of regret as he returned to his motorcar. Ginger smoothed out her skirt then stepped inside the club. She had every intention of just looking around and keeping her nose out of mischief when she spotted Thomas Friar.

She lifted her arm and waved a gloved hand. "Mr. Friar."

The club manager paused at the sound of his name, glanced at Ginger, pretended he hadn't seen her —which was simply ridiculous—and continued down the corridor. Unlike the gardener in the park, Ginger was fairly certain that Mr. Friar could hear perfectly well. She ran after him.

"Mr. Friar."

It appeared Thomas Friar had a shred of good manners left in him. He stopped, turned, and smiled. "Good afternoon, madam. If you have questions about our club, there is reading material at the front desk."

"Oh, I'd rather hear it from the horse's mouth." Ginger giggled. "I find boxing so intriguing. Do you box, Mr. Friar?" Ginger made a point of staring at the man's biceps. "You certainly look like you do."

"Well, yes, I do. I did. But now I manage the club. How can I help you, M—"

"Do women ever box?" Ginger purposely interrupted before she was forced to give away her identity.

"Women?" Mr. Friar scoffed aloud. "I hardly think that would be proper. I have to say it's a surprising question."

"I don't mean women boxing with men, but with other women. Why couldn't they, if they wanted to?"

Another snort from Mr. Friar was followed by, "Any woman who would want to fight is no woman at all."

Ginger's mind went to France and the times she had been trained in self-defence. She could hear her instructor, Captain Samson, his voice low and confident, in her head, "Keep your knees bent, legs slightly apart, and your hands up to protect your neck."

Mr. Friar seemed to notice Ginger's looks for the first time, his gaze resting on her face and then slowly scanning down to her shoes. Perhaps he imagined her in the ring wearing her underclothes. Reaching into his pocket, he removed a key and promptly unlocked his office door. "Why don't you come inside," he continued, lust dripping from each word. "I'd be happy to answer any questions you have."

As Ginger stepped into the office, she quickly noted everything inside, the furniture placement, the items on the desk, and the wall of dusty shelves filled with dusty trophies.

Adding a tinge of silliness to her voice, she said,

"Look at all these trophies! Did you win *all* of these, Mr. Friar?"

"Uh, well." The manager loosened his tie. "They're not mine, per se, but my fighters won them."

"Boxing is so beastly," Ginger said with a giggle. "You must make a lot of money. Enough to buy a motorcar, I bet."

Mr. Friar stood close to Ginger, the smell of cigarette smoke, body odour, and cheap hair oil assaulting her senses. "I haven't bought a new one yet, but I plan to soon." He smiled creepily. "Would you like that?"

Ginger laughed. "Of course. But that doesn't help right now. Are you sure you don't have a motorcar?"

"I got an old rattletrap, but it doesn't have the kind of space we'd need," Mr. Friar said. Then he made his first mistake. He ran a finger down Ginger's arm, and clasped her wrist.

Without even thinking, Ginger stepped back, twisted her waist to take a small step behind him, and firmly grasped her assailant's wrist. She had effectively twisted his arm behind him and forced him to bend forwards. With both of her hands, Ginger yanked the man's forearm up behind his back. It happened so fast that the manager gasped in surprise as much as in pain, as she held him there. He fell to one knee to alleviate the discomfort caused by her grip, but it was no use.

"Madam! Stop!"

"How about you answer a couple of questions first?"

"All right, what do you want to know?"

"Were you providing Marvin Elliot with cocaine?"

"What? No!"

"Where were you yesterday afternoon at two o'clock?"

"I don't know."

Ginger tightened her hold.

"I was here!" Mr. Friar spat. "What the blazes?"

"What do you know about the shooting?" Ginger asked calmly.

"Lester? Like I told the police, I was inside the club."

"Not Mr. Lester," Ginger explained patiently. "Marvin Elliot."

"What? Elliot was shot?"

"He was. Did you know?"

Thomas Friar's shoulders went slack. "No. Is he . . . ?"

"No, but it was close."

The sound of a throat clearing was followed by, "I see you've met my wife."

Ginger released her hold on Mr. Friar and smiled. "Oh hello, dear."

Mr. Friar hurried to his feet, blowing air through reddened cheeks as he fixed his tie. "This is your wife? She assaulted me. I could press charges!"

Ginger shrugged as Basil casually claimed a chair.

"Firstly, my wife does not 'assault' people; she does, however, defend herself if she is assaulted. So, if any pressing of charges is to be done, it shall not be by you. Secondly, I doubt you'd like word of this reaching the papers." Basil drew his finger through the air as if underlining a newspaper headline. "Former Boxer Is Brought To His Knees By A Lady."

Mr. Friar lowered himself into his chair, his face red with fury. Breathing heavily through his nose, he asked, "What do you want from me, Chief Inspector?"

Basil lifted his middle and index fingers. "In a matter of days, you're down two fighters."

"Rather rotten luck," Mr. Friar said with a snort.

"Bad luck comes with bad company," Basil said.

Mr. Friar narrowed his puffy eyes. "I don't know what you mean."

"I think you do," Basil returned. "Mortimer Sharp, for one."

"I told you. I don't really know the man."

"I have a witness who says you and Sharp have had meetings here in your office."

"I—"

"Mr. Friar!" Basil said sternly. "I suggest you start telling me the truth."

Mr. Friar slapped the top of his desk, taking his humiliation out on the furniture. "Look here! I didn't shoot anybody. Not Lester and not Elliot."

Ginger took a step towards the desk. "Do you provide cocaine to your fighters, Mr. Friar?"

"What?" Mr. Friar suddenly jerked his head. Then standing unnaturally still, he repeated, "What? Of course, I don't. Of course, I don't."

Ginger glanced at Basil, who subtly nodded, indicating he'd seen the same thing. Mr. Friar's change of behaviour indicated he was lying.

"Are you aware that Marvin Elliot may have been using cocaine?" Ginger asked.

"No, *Mrs. Reed*, but it wouldn't surprise me. Some fighters use it to help them in the ring. I was hoping Marvin wasn't doing that, though."

"So, you weren't supplying him?" Basil asked.

"I've already told you, sir, I don't supply drugs to anyone. You've got the wrong man Chief Inspector, and I resent the accusation."

"Have you ever used banned substances yourself?" Ginger asked. "Perhaps here in your office, even."

Mr. Friar breathed heavily, his shoulders rising. "What a ridiculous accusation."

"So, if a magistrate granted a search warrant, we wouldn't find anything?" Basil asked.

Thomas Friar threw his hands wide. "I have nothing to hide, Your Honour. That's what I would say to your magistrate."

"Elliot was starting to get quite vocal as time went on, wasn't he?" Basil pressed on. "The newspapers even called him *Marvin the Mouth*. People addicted to those substances often lose their ability to keep secrets, don't they? What secrets do you know, Mr. Friar?"

Mr. Friar flattened his palms on his desk and sprang to his feet. "If you weren't a copper, I would throw you out of here."

"But I *am* a policeman, Mr. Friar. If it is found that you are lying to me or withholding evidence, you will serve time at Wormwood Scrubs. Regarding your involvement with drugs here at your boxing club, I'm not currently investigating that specifically right now, but if I find that it played a role in the murder of Sid Lester and the attempted murder of Marvin Elliot..."

Thomas Friar worked his jaw before forcing himself to return to his seat. "Look here. Just to show you that I'm cooperating, I'll tell you something I'd normally keep under my hat."

"I'm eager to hear it," Basil said.

"If you want to go after someone who had some motive to kill Sid Lester, talk to Wiley Shaftoe."

"Marvin's corner coach?" Ginger said.

"He was Sid Lester's corner coach when Lester was just starting," Mr. Friar said. "The rumour is that when Lester started winning big, he abandoned old Shaftoe. Some say he didn't pay back a loan that Shaftoe had given him."

"You're saying that before Mr. Shaftoe was Marvin's corner man, he was on Sid Lester's team?" Ginger wanted to be sure she'd heard the man correctly.

"That's right." Once again, Mr. Friar pushed himself to his feet, but this time he leaned back, taking a less aggressive stance. "You've made a lot of accusations here today but very little in the way of proof of anything except what some person told you. If I were you, I would adjust your aim just a little. Now, if there's nothing else, I have work to do here."

"Thank you for your time," Basil said. He took Ginger's arm, and they left the bristly manager to stew over the interruption to his day.

19

As Ginger and Basil made their way down the corridor towards the back entrance, Ginger spotted Marvin's corner man stepping inside. "There's Wiley Shaftoe now." Raising her hand, she called out, "Mr. Shaftoe!"

Wiley Shaftoe stopped at the sound of her voice, squinted as he registered who'd spoken, then smiled. Removing his flat cap, he ran his hand over his greying, tightly curled hair. "Mrs. Reed, isn't it?"

"It is," Ginger said as they grouped together. "How are you?"

"Quite well, thank you," Mr. Shaftoe returned in his raspy voice. He extended his hand to Basil. "We met the night of the fight, though I didn't piece together that you two were married until after Mrs. Reed came to see me."

"Oh, yes," Ginger said. "I suppose I could have mentioned that my husband was a Chief Inspector."

"How do you do, Shaftoe," Basil said.

"How do you do," Mr. Shaftoe returned. Then, his expression grew sober. "Any news on Elliot?"

Ginger shook her head. "We've just come from the hospital. I'm afraid to report that there's been no change."

"I'm very sorry to hear that." Mr. Shaftoe looked up at the wall clock, then added, "It was good to see you again, but I must excuse myself. I'm running late for a sparring match."

"Would you mind if we came with you?" Basil said. "If you'd be so kind as to answer a few more questions."

"If you like," Mr. Shaftoe said as he began walking, "but I don't know what else I can tell you."

"It won't take long," Ginger added.

"All right, but I'll need to keep my eye on the ring. I'm training a new lad."

They entered the main auditorium of the gymnasium and were greeted by the smell of leather, sweat, and floor-cleaning solvent. About half a dozen men of various ages and sizes were dressed in trousers and vests, pounding heavy bags, skipping with a rope, or throwing heavy medicine balls. A few cast their glances towards Ginger, who, as a fashionably dressed lady, was the oddity in the room.

"My apologies, madam," Wiley Shaftoe said as he pointed at a long wooden bench against the far wall, across from the boxing ring. "The gymnasium isn't a proper setting for a lady such as yourself."

"I'm quite fine," Ginger said. "I assure you."

As all three took a seat on the bench, two burly young men climbed into the ring. They wore leather-padded head coverings that protected their foreheads and both sides of their jaws, along with large red, padded gloves.

"Go ahead, Eddy," Mr. Shaftoe said. "Fred can warm you up. I'll keep an eye on you."

The two men nodded, touched gloves together, and then shuffled around the ring.

"How long have you been Marvin Elliot's corner man?" Basil asked.

"Eight months." Mr. Shaftoe's eyes were on the ring. "Keep that right hand up, Eddy!"

"And how long did you work for Sid Lester?" Basil asked.

Mr. Shaftoe jerked, his neck twisting from the ring back to Basil. "*What?*"

"We've been told you once worked for Sid Lester," Ginger said. "Is that true?"

Mr. Shaftoe lowered his brown-eyed gaze to the floor. "Yes, it's true. But not for long, you see. Me and Lester didn't get on that well."

"How so?" Basil asked.

A shrug, then Mr. Shaftoe said, "He didn't like my coaching." Another shrug. "I moved on. It's all water under the bridge now."

"I suppose it is," Basil said, "with Lester being dead."

"I ain't got nothing to do with that, I swear."

"You didn't mention when we spoke," Ginger started, "that Sid Lester owed you money."

"Now see here. Who told you that?" Wiley Shaftoe said. "Friar?"

"Is it true?" Basil asked.

Wiley Shaftoe watched the sparring match for a moment before answering vaguely, "I loaned him a few quid."

"What did he need the money for?" Ginger asked.

"He said it was to pay his rent. He was behind a few months. This was before he was winning all his fights. At the time, he was all potential but no experience." He cupped one hand to his mouth and shouted towards the ring. "You're flat-footed, Eddy. You've got to jab and move, jab and move!"

"Do you think it really was for his rent?" Basil asked.

Mr. Shaftoe glanced back. "I had no reason to doubt it at the time."

"He was involved with dubious characters at that point, was he not?" Ginger said.

"If he was, I wouldn't have known it then." Mr. Shaftoe coughed into his hand. "Anyway, I told him he could pay me back when he started winning more often."

"But he didn't, did he?" Basil asked.

Wiley Shaftoe's jaw muscles clenched as he kept his eyes on the action in the ring. "Look. When I started training Sid Lester, no one knew anything about him. He was big and strong and had a jaw made of iron. But he was awkward in the ring. I taught him how to stay on his toes, protect himself, use his long reach, and read his opponent's rhythm. When he started winning, it was cos I gave him the tools he needed. So yeah, later, when he started making real money and ditched me, I was cross. It ain't about the money; it's about the humiliation."

He suddenly stood up and shouted angrily, "Darn it, Eddy, if you don't keep that right hand up, I'm going to get in that ring myself and show you what a real left hook feels like. Headgear or not!" He sat as he shouted, "C'mon, Fred. You're going too easy on him."

Fred touched a glove to his padded forehead and nodded, "All right, all right. I don't want to hurt the lad."

Folding his arms over his chest, Mr. Shaftoe continued, "I realised the best way to get revenge on Lester was to look for someone who could take him down. Someone younger, more intelligent, and faster. Someone who could humiliate Lester the way he humiliated me." He jabbed a finger in the air. "That's why I got behind Marvin Elliot. When I first saw him fight, I thought I had found someone with the talent to beat that big gorilla. Marvin had the speed and endurance. All he needed was someone to focus him, counter Lester's strong points and exploit his weak ones. And you saw it. I was right!" He clapped his hands together. "My revenge tasted pretty sweet, but it ended too quickly. I didn't count on Sid Lester failing to answer the bell."

"No one would've predicted that," Ginger said.

"After all those wins. And all that time in the limelight—" Wiley Shaftoe's gravelly voice lowered into a thick growl. "He was a coward in the end."

## 20

The next day, Ginger simply had to attend to her household and business affairs. Though she trusted Basil to successfully continue the investigation into Sid Lester's murder and Marvin's attack without her assistance, her mind had a hard time letting go. More than once, she mentally chastised herself for being distracted by the case when other pressing issues were at hand.

Having just fed Rosa, Ginger rocked the baby in the nursery.

"I've packed a trunk full of nappies and baby things," Nanny Green said. "I made sure to include clothing items suitable for all weather. Mrs. Beasley is making the bottles and necessary baby foods that will travel well. I assume you'll be taking the pram?"

Ginger was more than grateful for the nanny's help and her competent manner. "We will take the pram."

Even though they could easily purchase one in France, there would be a period leading to that event where not having a pram would prove to be an inconvenience. And since they were leaving in the morning, at short notice, there wasn't time to order one in advance.

As Ginger carefully extracted herself from the rocking chair, she placed her sleepy baby back into the crib. "Once you have Rosa's things sorted and packed, you must get yourself ready," Ginger said. Then, realising that she hadn't officially invited the nanny, she stared at the woman with a sense of alarm. "You are coming along, Abby, aren't you? I'm frightfully sorry that I haven't made my intention clear."

"It is rather short notice, madam."

"You shall be duly compensated."

"I hope you didn't think my hesitancy was related to that, madam," Nanny Green said. "Only, I don't know a word of French."

Ginger relaxed. Her nanny's reluctance was based on natural fears of leaving one's home. "You needn't worry," Ginger said. "I'm rather proficient with the French language, and you'll be travelling as part of our family. You will be safe and well cared for." Ginger inclined her head and added gently, "Besides, little Rosa would be lost without you."

Nanny Green put her shoulders back. "Of course. I'm dedicated to Rosa's welfare. The boat trip across the English Channel can't be very long."

"It's not long at all," Ginger said. "The trip will be

over before you know it. Now, I must see to my packing."

Ginger returned to her bedroom, where Lizzie was busy packing her trunks. A lady of her standing required many frocks and gowns, hats and gloves, and jewellery and make-up, as one never knew what kind of company one might keep while on the Continent. Certainly, once this case was solved and the danger to the family removed, it would be a cause for celebration, and Ginger anticipated, with great joy and eagerness, a time when she could host a big party at the French villa. She'd already rented the place and received a telegram confirming their registration that morning.

"Thank you, Lizzie," Ginger said upon inspecting the trunks and hat boxes. "Are you nearly ready to go yourself?" Ginger had remembered to inform her maid, who had been terribly excited about the prospects of travelling to the Continent, unlike the nanny.

"Very nearly, madam." Lizzie's pixie-like face was flushed with anticipation. "Once I've finished here, I'll do the last bits needed."

"Very good," Ginger said. "You seem to have all well underway. I have business to see to in my office. I shall be there should anyone want to see me."

Ginger ran into Ambrosia on the staircase—the dowager slowly making her way up as Ginger was rushing down. "Are you quite all right, Grandmother? You look a little peaky."

Holding on to the rail with one bejewelled hand

and her walking stick with the other, Ambrosia let out an exasperated breath. "There's so much activity in the house. Maids dashing to and fro, trunks and boxes being shuttled about. Felicia called in for a few moments, and the bustle was even too much for her."

"Felicia was here?"

"She gives her regards. I don't think she's excited about this sudden trip—her constitution isn't up for it."

"Oh mercy. Is she unwell again?"

Ambrosia nodded, her loose jowls jiggling. "Fatigued. And I sympathise. Is it really necessary that I go along on this impromptu journey? I'm advanced in years, as you know. I'm really not up for the excitement."

Ginger placed a hand on Ambrosia's arm. "You know I wouldn't ask this of you if I didn't think it was important. None of us is safe if we're not all safe."

"We've found the owner of the getaway motorcar!"

Basil eyed Braxton, who poked his head into his office just before tea break. A small pot of black tea was steeping on the desk before him.

Tea break would have to wait.

"Splendid!" Basil said as he stood. "Who's the owner?"

"According to the council register, the motorcar belongs to a William Kenmore of 235 Hawley Crescent."

"Billy Kenmore!" Basil's pulse sped at the news. "That's The Griffin's henchman. By Jove, we have him. With any luck, we'll be able to get Mortimer Sharp too. I believe Hawley Crescent is just over in Camden Town. Have you contacted the magistrate?"

"Yes, sir," Braxton said. "A signed warrant should be forthcoming in a few minutes."

An hour later, Basil parked his Austin in a middle-class city area. The address was part of a two-storey, red-bricked terraced housing block that looked well maintained with fresh white paint on the windowsills and doors. Basil looked for the blue Landaulette the gardener had seen, but neither that motorcar nor any with the matching number plate was in the area.

It was coming up on noon, and Basil hoped that Billy Kenmore was home. Perhaps in the act of counting illegal monies or drugs or doing something villainous.

Knocking produced no response. Basil let out a long sigh and motioned for Braxton to follow him back to his motorcar. "Perhaps we'll find him at the Windmill pub this time of day," Basil said.

"Excuse me, are you looking for Mr. Kenmore?"

Basil turned to the voice of a white-haired elderly woman standing in the house doorway next to Billy Kenmore's.

"Yes, we are, madam. I'm Chief Inspector Basil Reed from Scotland Yard, and this is Constable Braxton. And who might you be?"

"I'm Mrs. Dudley. I live next door." The lines of her heavily wrinkled face deepened into a scowl. "That man is trouble; I'll tell you that, Chief Inspector."

"Why would you say that?" Basil asked.

"Well, for one thing, he's very rude. A few days ago, he got into an argument with my husband Winston about rubbish collection or something ridiculous. Mr. Kenmore pushed my Winston! Seventy-four years old, and that lout pushed him down onto the ground, shouting and swearing. The neighbours on the other side saw it too. But that's not the worst of it."

"How so, madam?" Basil said with growing interest.

"When he pushed Winston, I saw a gun holster under his jacket. He has a gun."

"Have you seen anything else suspicious?" Braxton asked as he scribbled on his notepad.

The older woman narrowed heavily wrinkled eyes. "That's enough, isn't it?"

"Would you happen to know where he might be at this time of day?" Basil asked.

"I'd be glad to tell you, and I hope you arrest him on the spot for whatever he's done to cause the police to show up in my street."

Basil nodded. "That is indeed our intent, madam."

"My guess would be Shackleton's Billiard Hall, just a few streets down." Mrs. Dudley pointed a withered finger. "I've seen him coming and going from there a few times. It's across the road from the grocers."

Shackleton's Billiard Hall was on the ground floor of a four-storey building on the edge of Camden Town. Outside the front door, in plain view, was a blue 1924 Daimler D16 Landaulette with the number plate AL 6795.

"I have a feeling he might run," Basil said as he and Braxton stepped out of his Austin. "Position yourself around the back and be ready for him. I'll give you five minutes."

"Yes, sir," Braxton said, then jogged away.

Basil entered the smoke-filled billiard hall. At the end of the room, two men played at a table. A lean-looking man in his early thirties was leaning on a billiard cue, facing him. The man, already balding, was not familiar to Basil.

Bending over the table, lining up a shot, was Billy Kenmore. He wore a white long-sleeved shirt with a black waistcoat. A cigarette dangled from his mouth.

When the bald man noticed Basil heading towards them, he said something to Kenmore. Kenmore straightened, his expression growing slack.

The bald man stepped around to stand beside Kenmore.

"William Kenmore," Basil started, "I'm here to place you—"

Kenmore violently pushed the bald man towards Basil, knocking Basil against the edge of the billiard table. As Basil untangled himself from the startled bald man, Kenmore threw his cue like a spear. Basil ducked, avoiding the wooden missile just in time.

"Stop there, Kenmore!" Basil shouted as The Griffin's henchman ran towards a rear hallway with a sign indicating where the water closets were. Basil raced after him, hoping he could corner him there, but as Kenmore rounded the corner, he crashed against an exit door.

Basil emerged from the rear of the building, dodging overturned dustbins, relieved to find Braxton pinning Kenmore against the rear brick wall of the building. The henchman's arm was twisted up behind his back, and his face pressed against the wall as Braxton gripped the back of his head.

"Good work, Braxton," Basil said, slightly out of breath. "Now, as I was saying, William Kenmore, I hereby place you under arrest for the murder of Sid Lester."

## 21

Basil waited two hours before he ordered Billy Kenmore to be taken for interrogation. He wanted him to sit in a holding cell long enough to realise the implications—namely, he was firmly in custody and would soon be charged with murder. Basil suspected that Kenmore had been ordered to kill Sid Lester by Mortimer Sharp. The goal was to convince Kenmore to turn on The Griffin and be willing to testify against him.

"I told yer, I was in the boxin' club when Sid Lester was shot!" Kenmore said when Basil, along with Braxton, entered the room.

Kenmore sat on the far side of a wooden table with his hands cuffed behind his back. The room was sparse, with a single lamp hanging from the ceiling. Basil sat across from the man while Braxton leaned against the closed door.

"Unfortunately for you," Basil started, "that's a weak alibi."

"What d'yer mean?" Kenmore shifted awkwardly. "There were witnesses!"

"There were indeed," Basil said. "We got a list of them all from Thomas Friar. Although it took the police time to question them, we can't find one person who could decisively say what time you left the building or if you were still watching the exhibition fight when the shooting took place. As you know, the door to the alley isn't visible from the main auditorium. It would've been easy to slip out, get in your motorcar, and shoot Sid Lester as he left. I think you were there, waiting for him. I'm told the fighters come the next day to collect their winnings, and you relied on Lester doing just that."

Kenmore's eyes glistened like a man who had a secret. "I dinn't kill Lester. You 'ave the wrong man."

"Then why did you run from me at the billiard hall?" Basil asked.

Kenmore shrugged. "I don't trust yer. I don't trust any coppers. There's been a murder at the boxin' club, and from what I 'ear, someone tried to kill Elliot. That's enough to make coppers like you desperate to arrest somebody. If I 'ad my choice, I'd rather not sit in a jail cell whilst the real killer struts about free as a bird."

"You were arrested five years ago on charges of assault," Basil said. "We looked up your records."

"Yeah, so? I spent eight months in prison for somethin' that wasn't my fault."

"The magistrate certainly thought it was."

"They said I attacked someone in a pub." Kenmore snarled. "The bloke was having a go at me."

"Witnesses said you attacked the man without provocation," Basil said. "You had brass knuckles in your pocket. You broke his jaw and two of his ribs."

"'E was bigger than me. It was self-defence!"

"Uh-huh." Basil shot a glance at Braxton.

"There, yer see? You don't believe me either. 'Ow's a poor bloke like me supposed to trust the coppers when they never believe a word I say?"

"I suspect that the man owed money to Sharp," Basil said. "Were you answering to him at the time?"

Shaking his head as if the question was ridiculous, Kenmore scowled. "No."

"What kind of work do you do for Sharp now?" Basil asked.

Kenmore flashed a sloppy smile. "I make sure 'is clothes get washed."

"Where were you yesterday at two in the afternoon?"

"I was playin' billiards."

"With whom?"

"Various people."

"Names, Mr. Kenmore."

"Well, Victor Price, for one. The bloke you saw me

with today. He's easy to find; he plays there almost every day."

Basil glanced at Braxton, ensuring his constable was busy writing everything down. Confident, he pressed Kenmore harder.

"Look, Kenmore, we know how Lester quit the fight early and that certain people would be hurt by him short-circuiting his career like that. We know he was to be made an example of. We know who ordered the killing. Admit that Mortimer Sharp ordered you to kill Sid Lester, and we'll make sure the magistrate knows you helped us." Basil held the man's squinty glare. "I'm not as interested in you as I am in him."

"What a relief!" Kenmore said sarcastically. "By the way, 'ow's your lovely family doin' these days?"

Kenmore's snide smile made Basil want to lunge at him from across the table, but he kept his composure and his voice even. "Give us what we want, Kenmore, and things will go better for you. I won't offer again."

"So, you want me to say Sharp ordered me to kill Lester?"

"Yes."

Kenmore burst out laughing. "You 'ave nothin'. All you 'ave are your suspicions and theories. Nothin' to link me to anythin'. You must think I'm an idiot."

"You're the registered owner of a 1924 Daimler D16 Landaulette," Basil said matter-of-factly.

"Yeah. So what?"

"A shiny royal blue." He turned to Braxton, who

was busy scribbling notes in his notepad. "That's a nice motorcar, isn't it, Constable Braxton?"

"Indeed, sir," Braxton said. "I think I need to change careers. Seems to be a lot of money in laundry services for gang bosses."

Kenmore shot Braxton a withering look.

"The registration number is AL 6795," Basil continued as he turned back to Kenmore. "You want to know how I know that?"

"I bet he does," Braxton said.

Kenmore stared hard at Basil with his eyebrows furrowed. "I suppose you could 'ave checked with the council register."

"True. I have done that. I also have a witness who saw that motorcar driving out of that alley at the exact time of the shooting."

The sneer fell off Kenmore's face.

"You almost ran him over, but you didn't see him, did you?" Basil said. "You were looking in the rearview mirror as you roared out of the alley. Fortunately, the man had his wits about him, and after dodging out of the way, he wrote down your motorcar make and registration number."

The room was dead silent for a long moment. Then Kenmore growled, "I want my solicitor."

GINGER REGRETTED the extra stress and anxiety she'd placed on Ambrosia and Felicia, but it couldn't be helped. In her years of solving mysteries, many of them murders, never once had she or her family become a personal target.

Technically, Basil's nemesis had become her own, but one had to take the good and the bad in marriage.

Mortimer Sharp was an anomaly. They simply had to stop him and all would be well in their Reed family household once again.

Stepping into her study, Ginger noticed the empty dog bed, making her think of Boss and Scout. Where were those two? She pivoted and headed for the kitchen.

"They were here," Mrs. Beasley explained with a note of disapproval in her voice. "Snatched a couple of biscuits and headed outside."

Once Scout's tutor had been released from his duties, Scout had been instructed to pack his things. Ginger hardly believed her son had accomplished his task so quickly, but then again, what did a thirteen-year-old boy need besides a collection of shorts, shirts, and trousers? Hopefully, a book or two and perhaps a ball and cricket bat.

Ginger was pretty sure she'd find the boy and the dog in the stable, and after a short trek through the back garden, her hypothesis was proven correct. Scout was brushing down Ginger's gelding, Goldmine.

"I thought I'd find you two here," she said as she entered.

At the sound of her voice, Boss scampered to her,

and Ginger scooped him into her arms. "Hey there, Bossy. Are you and Scout keeping out of trouble?"

Without losing his stroking rhythm, Scout said, "Hello, Mum."

"Are you packed?" Ginger asked. "We're leaving first thing in the morning."

"I'm ready. I'm just saying goodbye to Goldmine and Sir Blackwell." He paused and stared at Ginger. "Are they going to be all right? I take care of them every day, you know."

"I do know that," Ginger said. "It's what makes you such a terrific horseman. Clement will take good care of them."

"But—"

"Clement took care of Goldmine before you were here to do it," Ginger reminded Scout gently. "And we won't be gone very long."

"How long?"

"Perhaps a month. No more than two."

"A *whole* month?"

"It sounds like a long time, but it'll go by quickly. Time always does when you visit a new country. There's so much new to see and do. And wait until you taste French pastries!"

"I suppose so," Scout said, relenting. "At least I'll have Boss with me, won't I?"

Ginger set Boss back on the ground, and he returned to a spot in the hay where he'd made himself a bed. "You certainly will," Ginger said. "Now, are you sure you've packed everything? Including the schoolwork Mr. Fulton has assigned? Make sure you don't forget that."

Scout's shoulders slumped. "Yes, Mum."

Satisfied, Ginger headed back inside. On seeing Pippins, she stopped her butler to give him a small task. "Please send a message to Lady Davenport-Witt enquiring of her health and asking if there is anything she needs from me."

Pippins bowed his bald head. "Certainly, madam."

When Ginger finally made it to her study, she found that the morning chores had already exhausted her, and once at her desk rang the bell for tea. Grace, the kitchen maid, responded, and Ginger made her request.

"Would you like a sandwich or biscuits to go with that, madam?"

Ginger was about to say no when she realised she felt a bit peckish. "Actually, an egg and watercress sandwich would be delightful."

Finally, she could pay attention to the pile of paperwork on her desk, including the post stacked dreadfully high. She'd already alerted Madame Roux, and Ginger was grateful that her manager was more than competent to run the shop in her absence. Grace returned with her tea and sandwiches, and Ginger continued to answer the post, take telephone calls, and make notes for Madame Roux as she sipped and nibbled.

Despite her occupation with the current work-related tasks, Ginger's mind still flitted to the case. How was Basil doing? Had he found the owner of the getaway motorcar? She hadn't heard from him at all that morning. Was he all right?

She thought about the interviews they'd conducted the day before with Wiley Shaftoe and Thomas Friar. Then she considered the mysterious door in the alley and the man in the wheelchair who had stared at her.

*And Marvin.*

*Poor Marvin.* Ginger had rung up the hospital first thing in the morning, and the news was unchanged. She'd sneak a visit to see him before leaving for France. Ginger finished with the post, her work for Feathers & Flair, and then prepared a telegram to Haley. She'd meant to do it earlier, but the morning had gotten away from her.

In the briefest of terms, lest the message somehow got intercepted, Ginger informed Haley she could expect company in the near future and that she would contact her with more information shortly. With that, she set off to find Pippins.

"Pippins?"

The butler, with that magical sense he seemed to possess, appeared. "Madam?"

"Would you ask Lizzie or Grace to run to the telegraph office?"

"Yes, madam," Pippin said, taking the message from Ginger.

Her office telephone rang, and Pippins discreetly left her alone. She picked up the receiver and the operator connected her to her call. Basil was on the line.

"What is it love?" she asked.

"Marvin has awakened," Basil returned. "He remembers nothing. Can you meet me at the hospital in an hour?"

22

Basil and Ginger stood at the foot of Marvin's hospital bed with its white pipe-and-bar frame. Basil, for his part, was again struck by the contrast that such a short time could bring. Just yesterday, he'd stood on that same spot, struggling with the feeling he was staring at a corpse. Marvin had been unmoving, pale, and seemed to hover in that shadowland between the realm of the living and the grave. Significant colour had returned to his cheeks. Fewer bandages were wrapped around his head, allowing wisps of hair to poke out from the cotton gauze.

"Good afternoon." The same doctor they had encountered before, a tall middle-aged man with a full head of greying hair and black-framed spectacles, walked in wearing a white doctor's coat. "You two are the relatives who visited yesterday." He nodded at

Basil. "You're from Scotland Yard if I remember correctly."

"Yes, indeed," Basil said.

Ginger went immediately to Marvin's side. "How are you feeling, Marvin?"

"My 'ead 'urts like the blazes." His voice was slurred, and he only used one side of his mouth. He tried to raise his left arm, but failed, then wiggled two fingers instead. "I can't move me arm."

"That's all right," Ginger returned gently. "You just rest quietly and allow your body to heal. Mr. Reed and I are going to step out to speak to the doctor. We'll be right back."

In the corridor, Basil nodded to the officer who stood on duty. "Good afternoon, Constable Fletcher."

"Sir," the constable returned. The man had a slender face and eyes that darted about in a way that made Ginger uneasy.

After stepping out of the policeman's hearing, Basil said, "Doctor, what can you tell us?"

"Mr. Elliot's vital signs are normal, and his wound is healing nicely. The bullet, as you know, made a clean exit." Clearing his throat, the doctor continued. "However, a certain degree of brain damage has been detected. You would have noticed evidence of it when Mr. Elliot spoke. And his short-term memory is gone, but he should be able to retain any new memories he'll make going forward."

"Will this be permanent?" Ginger asked.

"He'll never box again if that's what you're asking, not with the damage affecting his arms," the doctor said. "With treatment, he should be capable of simple tasks." He offered an encouraging smile. "He's very fortunate to be alive."

Basil glanced at the door behind which Marvin lay in his hospital bed. What would Marvin do if he had lost his ability to make his own living? An image of the tramps on the street begging for pennies, holding their hats out to strangers, flashed across his mind.

"Doctor," he started, "I'd appreciate it if you could keep Mr. Elliot's awakened condition a secret for now. Until we've concluded our investigation."

"Certainly. You have my word on that," the doctor said before returning to the nurses' desk.

Basil and Ginger returned to Marvin, who was pushing away his tray of dirty dishes, which were scraped clean.

"Oh 'ello," he said as if seeing them for the first time. "Nice of yer to come and see me."

"Marvin," Ginger said. "We were here a few minutes ago."

Marvin's brow furrowed, confusion evident in eyes that were suddenly childlike, with the left one drooping in a concerning manner.

"I dun't remember that, madam."

"The doctor said you'll have trouble with your memory for a while," Ginger said. "It's quite normal."

"What do you remember?" Basil asked.

Marvin slowly shook his head, then winced. "Not much. I was shoppin' for tabacca. Then suddenly I wake up 'ere."

"Do you know what happened to you?" Ginger asked.

Marvin's right hand moved to his head. "I 'urt meself."

Basil held in a frustrated breath. He'd hoped that Marvin could identify his attacker, that he'd offer some kind of clue. But if he had to go by the doctor's prognosis, he'd never remember the day of the attack.

A young, pretty nurse popped her head around the door.

"Good afternoon," she said. "Just checking up on our patient." She stepped to Marvin's side. "Is there anything I can do for you, Mr. Elliot?" she asked warmly.

Marvin gaped at the pretty nurse, but no sound left his mouth.

"How about we fluff up your pillow?" The nurse carefully reached around Marvin's head and adjusted the slender pillow. "Here now," she said. "What's this?" In her hand was a small white envelope that had apparently been slipped underneath it. The nurse chuckled and held up the note. "Is this for me?"

Marvin winced as he made the motion to shake his head.

The nurse examined the envelope. "It's sealed and

addressed to a Chief Inspector Reed." She looked at Basil. "Do you know who that is?"

Basil held out his hand. "That's me. Thank you."

He waited for the nurse to leave them alone before opening the envelope. His blood ran cold when he saw the sharp, left-leaning handwriting. He had seen it before.

He handed it to Ginger, and her green eyes darkened as she read.

*A fighter with no fight. A warrior who cannot make war...*
*Whilst I can strike if I like.*
*Or not.*

Basil emitted a soft groan.

Once they were in the corridor, Basil immediately called the officer on duty aside.

"Constable Fletcher, did Mr. Elliot have any visitors today besides Mrs. Reed and me?"

The officer, with wide, serious eyes, shook his head. "No, sir. I was told no visitors under any circumstances."

"No one besides the nurses, doctors, and us are allowed into that room," Basil said sternly. "Is that understood?"

"Yes, sir."

Basil used the nurses' station telephone to ring the

Yard, instructing another officer to come to the hospital pronto. "I'll not leave until one arrives," he said.

Ginger was already seated on one of the visitors' chairs in the corridor when he joined her. He let out a disgruntled sigh as he settled into the seat beside his wife. "How did he do it? How did The Griffin get past the officer on duty?"

"Perhaps he has a doctor, nurse, or orderly on his payroll," Ginger said. "Or . . . even a policeman."

Basil shot Ginger a look. He wished he could defend the Metropolitan Police, but no organisation could boast zero corruption in its ranks. As much as Basil hated to think about it, there could be a bad copper in Mortimer Sharp's pocket.

Basil took Ginger's hand. "You don't need to wait here with me. I'll stay until I'm assured of Marvin's safety."

Ginger looked as if she was about to protest, but then her gaze dropped to the floor.

"Actually, if you don't mind, love," she said. "I have a frightful amount to do to prepare for France, and I should check up on Magna before I go."


As Ginger travelled in the back of a black taxicab towards Watson Street in the West End, her mind replayed the recent events at the hospital. The good news was that Marvin had survived his attack and had come out of his coma. The bad news was the gunshot had brought on stroke-like symptoms. Ginger didn't have time to consider the ramifications of that right now. The pressing problem was Marvin's continued safety. It was one thing for Basil to arrange for police protection while Marvin lay in a private room in the hospital and quite another for when the time came and the doctor released him to go home.

Reaching the office of Lady Gold Investigations, Ginger released a soft sigh of relief when she saw the interior electric light shining through the window. It meant that Magna Jones was on the premises. Ginger was eager to discuss this case with someone with a bit of objectivity.

The bell over the door announced Ginger's arrival. Magna rose from the chair at Felicia's old desk and stared towards the doorway with a look of anticipation that fell away immediately when she saw it was Ginger.

"Ah, it's you," Magna said. "Coming to check up on me?"

Ginger removed her gloves, slipped them into her handbag, which she set on a side table, and hung her coat on the rack. "And what if I was," she said.

Magna lifted a slender shoulder. "I would be disappointed if you didn't. Coffee? It's freshly brewed, more or less."

"I can't stay long," Ginger said, "but I think I shall since it's already made. Don't trouble yourself. I can get it."

Today Magna wore another dark dress suit, similar to the last one, and Ginger presumed it was the woman's preferred uniform. Simple and unassuming.

"Please allow me," Magna said. "I am the employee, after all."

After her experience with Magna during the war, Ginger would never see herself as over Magna in any way; however, if this was how Magna wanted to play it, she wouldn't create a fuss.

Magna returned with two cups of steaming, dark coffee. "Two sugars for you," she said.

Ginger eyed her old colleague over the rim of her cup as she took a sip. Magna did the same. They were like two wild animals circling each other, instinctively knowing they needed each other to forage food, yet suspicious that one might become the meal for the other.

"Did I miss anything whilst I was gone?" Ginger finally asked.

"Not a lot. I went through the files to familiarise myself with the cases that have come through this office. And sorted the post. A telephone call came in from someone needing a signature from an estranged spouse to prove they have grounds for divorce. Apparently, his wife had a history of being disagreeable." Magna set her coffee cup down on a ceramic coaster. "Don't worry. I took care of it."

Ginger didn't doubt Magna's competence in the slightest.

"Is there something you'd like me to do for you?" Magna said. "Beyond filing and making coffee."

"Actually," Ginger started, "there is something. There's a police officer. Now, I normally like to believe the best and tend to give people the benefit of the doubt."

"What's his name?"

"Nigel Fletcher."

Magna jotted the name on a pad of paper. "Leave it to me."

"All right." Ginger sipped her coffee, feeling a little unnerved. "Just to clarify, I want him to keep breathing."

"Ha!" Magna snorted as she laughed. "I'm not an assassin, Ginger. Unless . . ." she winked.

*Oh mercy.* Ginger wondered if she'd inadvertently hired a dangerous weapon. The war had done terrible things to the minds of many soldiers who fought and agents who had gone on dangerous missions. Was Magna Jones troubled? If so, how much?

Magna cocked her head as her dark eyes narrowed. "If there's anything questionable in this man's life, I'll find it. If he doesn't live to confirm it, it won't be because of me."

"Good."

The bell over the door rang, and to Ginger's surprise, Colin Venables entered the office.

"Good afternoon," he said without looking their way. Instead, his eyes darted about, scanning the perimeter of the space, the walls, the ceilings, and the floor.

Ginger got to her feet. "Can I help you?"

"I'm just reminiscin'," Mr. Venables said as he removed his hat. "This was once my family business." Ginger noted his quivering fingers. Were his memories upsetting?

"The cobblers?" Ginger asked.

"Yes. My father and grandfather both. Excellent cobblers." He pushed up his spectacles as he added, "Unfortunately, the talent didn't come down to me or my brother. After the war, well, it was just time to let it go." Finally, his eyes settled on Ginger and flashed with recognition. "Mrs. Reed?"

"Yes." Ginger held out a hand. "I don't believe we've met."

"No," Mr. Venables said, taking her hand. "But I've seen your photograph in the newspapers a few times. You're the former Lady Gold."

Ginger smiled. "Of Lady Gold Investigations."

Colin Venables snapped his fingers. "Capital!" His gaze moved to Magna.

"This is my assistant," Ginger said. "Miss Jones."

Magna didn't get to her feet or offer her hand. Mr. Venables nodded his head. "Good day, Miss Jones."

"Are you in need of investigative services?" Ginger asked.

Mr. Venables' expression widened in surprise.

"From a couple of ladies?" He sniffed, then added, "I should think not."

Ginger forced a smile. "You're only here to reminisce?"

Mr. Venables choosing now of all times to call, just as he was connected with a murder investigation, would be quite a coincidence.

Ginger didn't believe in coincidences. So why would Mr. Venables be following her?

"Yes, indeed," Mr. Venables said. "I'm terribly sorry to have interrupted you. I'm sure you have many gossipy tea-party scandals to deal with. Good day." He returned his hat to his head as he left.

Ginger lowered herself back in her chair. When she turned to Magna, her assistant was scowling.

"Would you like me to look into him as well?" Magna asked.

Ginger pushed a lock of hair behind her ear. "Yes, please do."

## 23

The next morning, Hartigan House was a hive of activity. The luggage sitting in the entrance hall would require at least three taxicabs to shuttle, and Ginger didn't doubt that Felicia had nearly as much waiting across the cul-de-sac.

Scout sat on the steps with Boss at his feet and a frown on his face. He was not only disgruntled that he wasn't allowed to visit Marvin in the hospital, but the lad was also convinced that he'd hate France since he'd disliked learning the language. And he didn't want to leave the horses. Ginger believed it was more of a heart issue than trust. Scout would miss the horses, and that was the truth of it.

Ambrosia had been ready since early that morning, waiting primly in the drawing room for departure. She fussed about having to travel at her age, but Ginger caught the glimmer of excitement in her rheumy eyes.

Ambrosia hadn't been to France since long before the war, and Ginger believed she was secretly looking forward to returning.

Lizzie and Langley, Ginger and Ambrosia's maids, bustled about with last-minute items as Pippins hovered about waiting for instructions. There wasn't much for her butler to do when their large party was about to leave besides saying goodbye and securing the doors and windows once everyone had left.

Rocking Rosa gently in the pram, Nanny Green had the baby bundled up and ready to go. The bassinet would be removed from the apparatus at the train station and carried on to the train for Rosa to sleep in. The frame would go to the baggage van with the rest of the trunks.

Ginger wore an emerald-green frock with a matching jacket, a perfect ensemble for travelling. In her handbag was *The Great Gatsby* to help her pass the time. Crossing the English Channel might make her homesick for America.

Pippins was quick to answer a knock on the door, and Ginger wondered if the taxicabs had arrived, but instead, Charles entered.

"Good morning," he said. "Is everyone nearly ready?"

"I believe so," Ginger replied. "The taxicabs should arrive shortly. How is Felicia?"

"She doesn't want to think about why we're leaving on this impromptu 'holiday'," Charles said. "She's keeping her mind occupied with the shopping she plans to do in Paris."

Ginger smiled. "I'm also looking forward to that part of our adventure."

The sound of a motor engine prompted Charles to glance out the window. "The taxicabs are here." He opened the door to usher the drivers inside so they could collect the luggage.

Ginger headed across the court to check on Felicia. Burton, the Davenport-Witt butler who doubled as Charles' valet, had noticed the taxicabs' arrival and directed the drivers to pick up the suitcases. Burton was coming to France to attend to Charles and to add another man to the group. With only Felicia and Charles—along with Felicia's maid Daphne and Burton—making the journey from the Davenport-Witt household, their luggage collection was slightly smaller.

"Felicia, darling," Ginger started when she approached. "How are you this morning?"

"If you're asking about my daily ailment," Felicia said. "It remains quite improved. I'm just a little tired. I'm grateful, as I could hardly imagine traversing the Channel otherwise."

"I'm relieved as well," Ginger said. "Once we're on the Continent, things shall be much easier and more enjoyable."

Felicia gazed about nervously. "I understand the impetus for this rushed itinerary, but if we're truly in danger, what's stopping our nemesis from following us to the train station? Or onto France, for that matter?"

Ginger wasn't surprised by the question. Felicia had worked for her as an assistant at Lady Gold Investigations for two years and was a clever mystery author. It would be more surprising if she *didn't* think of such things.

"Basil has undercover men watching," Ginger said. "If they see anyone suspicious milling about, they will apprehend them for questioning. Besides, this is why we're leaving so quickly, without a chance for gossipers to get the word out. When anyone notices that we're gone, we'll be far away. The staff has been instructed to say we've gone to America."

"I should've known you've thought of everything, Ginger," Felicia said.

Charles stepped inside and picked up the last of their bags. "Are you ladies ready to go?"

"We are," Ginger said, stepping out ahead of them. "*Allons-y!*"

The convoy of taxicabs delivered the Reeds, Davenport-Witts, the Dowager Lady Gold, and their accompanying entourage to Waterloo station promptly. Ginger kept a lookout for Basil, who'd promised to meet them there to say his goodbyes and send them off. She understood why he had to stay behind. At this point, the Yard couldn't give this case to a new inspector and trust he would solve the case and apprehend Mortimer Sharp. No, this was something that they needed to ensure was done and done right. Ginger wished she could stay in London to assist, but Basil insisted that she go. The family needed her.

The train to Dover arrived. Charles saw to the luggage, ensuring it all got into the baggage van in an organised manner. Ginger kept her crew together, holding Rosa in her arms and watching Scout with Boss on a leash. They were eleven with the children, the nanny, three maids, one butler, Ambrosia, Felicia, Charles, and herself.

The whistle blew, warning the travellers the train was about to depart.

"Where's Basil?" Felicia asked. "I thought he was seeing us off."

Ginger scanned the faces on the platform, her nerves tightening when her eyes didn't land on a familiar face. "I don't know," she said. "Perhaps he's caught in traffic."

A second whistle prompted stragglers to hurry on board. Felicia assisted Ambrosia, Scout, and Boss. Rosa was safely in the care of the nanny. And the staff left for the second-class carriage.

Ginger waited on the platform for Charles' return from overseeing the luggage. Her eyes scanned for signs of disruption or anything out of the ordinary. She hoped Basil would push through the mass to say goodbye as he'd promised.

A dark-haired woman with steely eyes and a determined gait broke through the meandering crowd and headed for Ginger.

Alarm filled Ginger's chest. "Magna? What are you doing here?"

"I have a message from Mr. Reed."

"Where is he?" Ginger asked quickly. "Is he all right?"

"He's fine. But he has a message. He rang me at the office and asked me to let you know he can't make it in time to see you off."

"Did he say why?"

"He prefaced his message by saying he didn't want you to worry."

"Now I'm really worried."

"There's been another murder at the boxing club," Magna said.

*Oh mercy.*

"Did he say who?"

"No. He said he'd send a telegram to you in France."

Ginger worked her lips. Another murder at the boxing club? It had to be related to the Sid Lester case and probably the attack on Marvin's life.

"Is there anything else?" Ginger asked.

"Yes. I looked into Colin Venables. It turns out he's Richard Venables' brother, the owner of Regency Eatery."

"The fellow in the wheelchair?"

Magna nodded. "Perhaps not essential information

until you consider this: Richard Venables was put into the wheelchair by Sid Lester."

Ginger's mind was a whirlwind. Had Colin Venables killed Sid Lester in revenge for putting his brother in a wheelchair?

And who was this latest murder victim? Just how dangerous was Colin Venables?

Charles arrived just as the conductor blew the whistle to warn of the impending departure and the coach attendant yelled, "All aboard!"

Ginger grabbed Charles' arm. "I'm staying, Charles."

Startled, Charles sputtered, "W-what?"

Ginger pushed him to the carriage, which was already in motion. "You can't miss the train, Charles! Go. I promise I'll meet up with you all at the weekend."

## 24

The bloodied form of Jimmy Willis, his unruly white hair matted with blood and dirt, lay face down about thirty feet from the alley door leading to the park adjacent to the boxing club. Photographs were taken, and the area around the body was measured and recorded. Dr. Gupta knelt beside Willis.

"Did you know him, Chief Inspector?" Dr. Gupta asked without looking up.

"He was Sid Lester's cornerman," Basil said. He scanned the area, noting the back side of the building that butted up against the park, and a collection of residences and places of business, the Regency Eatery included. The park wasn't as well tended at this end, with prominent brush and weeds along the path. The mystery door he and Ginger had found that opened to the park from the alley behind the boxing club had been found standing ajar.

Braxton, who'd accompanied Basil on the call, said, "Looks like he might have been running from someone."

Basil nodded. Jimmy Willis worked at the boxing club next door, so his presence in this area of town was expected. However, when he and Ginger had examined the door in the brick wall, it had been nearly camouflaged with vines and dried leaves, clearly not used in recent times . . . until now. The question was, who was Willis running from and why?

Dr. Gupta straightened up. "He was shot through the heart from the back. He died instantly."

"Is there an exit wound?" Basil asked.

"No, I think the bullet is still in there."

"How about time of death?"

"Judging by the fact that there's still some moisture under the eyelids, the body temperature is still higher than ambient conditions, and those little blighters haven't yet invaded . . ." He pointed to a small ant hill about fifteen feet away. "I would say not more than two hours ago."

"Excellent, Doctor," Basil said, checking his watch. It was almost nine a.m.

A beat officer had called the death in after being tracked down by a witness.

Basil turned to Braxton. "Do we know who the

witness is yet? Have you spoken to the coppers on duty?"

"Yes, sir," Braxton said, referring to his notes. "It was a cook from the Regency Eatery."

Basil's gaze darted to the blue-copper roof and the small patio at the back of the premises.

"Did the cook see what happened?" Basil asked.

"No. He went to find the policeman on behalf of the owner who was the one who saw it."

"Gather a few men and start canvassing the area. Interview the inhabitants surrounding the park, including anyone who might have been at the boxing club. I want to know why Jimmy Willis was here at this time of the morning and who the last person was to see him alive."

Basil looked at his watch while his mouth formed a tight line. Right now, his family was well on the way to Dover, having left Waterloo station. They would be on the afternoon ferry to Calais in a few more hours. The thought was both comforting and disquieting. He regretted missing his promised send-off.

Squaring his shoulders, he slowly walked along the path Jimmy Willis must have taken to where he now lay. He scoured the freshly cut grass for signs of a spent bullet casing, which would help determine where the killer had stood when he took his shot.

Having found nothing in the grass, Basil removed a magnifying glass from his suit pocket and examined the area around a nearby elm tree, a search that turned out to be unproductive. Returning to the door, he pulled on the knob. It moved stubbornly, with a protesting creak. Basil stepped into the brick-wall-enclosed alleyway behind the boxing club and carefully examined the threshold and cobblestone floor close to the wall. Lying up against the brick was a single brass casing. Basil picked it up with gloved hands and examined it with his magnifying glass.

Just that morning, as Basil had arrived at his office, he'd found a report from the forensics lab lying on his desk. The report contained results from a technician and a firearms expert who had both closely examined the casings found at the Sid Lester shooting and the one at Marvin's flat. Employing a new invention, the comparison microscope, it was determined that the Sid Lester gunman employed a Colt forty-five. The Colt Company made their pistols with a left twist inside the barrel, often leaving markings on the cartridge. All other pistols were manufactured with right-hand twists.

The cartridge found at Marvin's flat was a nine millimetre and had a right-hand twist; however, because it was made to metric measurements, it was a European make, probably German. The firearms' expert was reasonably sure that it came from a German Parabellum semi-automatic pistol, more recently known as a Luger. The gun was not commonly found in Britain and was known for its elegant design and exceptional accuracy. It was also quite expensive compared with more commonly found models such as the American-made Colt or British-made Webley.

The conclusion was that two weapons were used, and the standard conclusion would be that the two events, the Lester murder and Marvin's attack, were not connected.

Basil's gut was telling him otherwise.

He stepped back through the door and counted off the paces to the body lying in the grass. "Fourteen paces," he said to Dr. Gupta.

They both looked at the door and then back down at the body.

"It appears the killer is a decent marksman to manage shooting someone through the heart with a short-barrel weapon like a pistol," Dr. Gupta returned.

A shadow filled the door leading to the alley, and Basil assumed ambulance services had arrived. He glanced over to greet the attendant, then froze.

"Ginger?" he said. His face tightened with disapproval. "What on earth are you doing here?"

GINGER WAS USED to warmer greetings from her husband, but in this circumstance, she allowed for his brashness.

"Hello, love! This *is* a surprise, I know. I can explain, but first—" Ginger stepped aside to allow her companion to step through the doorway and into the park. "Allow me to introduce my new assistant, Miss Magna Jones."

Basil was nothing if not a gentleman. He reached out his hand to Magna. "How do you do, Miss Jones. It's nice to finally meet you in person." He gave her a grim look. "I see you delivered my message. However, I had expected my wife to get on the train."

Ginger chuckled as she patted Basil's arm. "You mustn't blame her, love. It was entirely my idea." She stretched out an arm to wave to the pathologist, the sleeve of her frock catching in the breeze. "Good morning, Dr. Gupta."

"Good morning, Mrs. Reed," Dr. Gupta said with a smile. "It's always a pleasure."

"This is my new assistant, Miss Jones," Ginger added politely. "We met working on the telephones in France during the war. Magna, Dr. Gupta is one of London's finest pathologists. He's blessed with a lovely wife and child."

Ginger added the last part because Dr. Manu Gupta was rather attractive, and, as far as Ginger knew, Magna was unattached.

Dr. Gupta ducked his chin. "Pleased to meet you, Miss Jones."

Not even the handsome doctor's charm could produce a smile from Magna Jones. "Likewise," she said before focusing back on the body.

Ginger stepped closer to the corpse. "Now, who do we have here?"

"Jimmy Willis," Basil said.

"Sid Lester's trainer?" Ginger asked.

Basil nodded. "Indeed. It appears he was running from someone, came through the door, and was shot in the back." He lowered his voice, directing it at Ginger. "Now, are you going to tell me why you're not on a train to Dover with the rest of our family?"

"Of course. Magna came to deliver your message, but she also brought news regarding Colin Venables. You see, he called in at Lady Gold Investigations yesterday. Apparently, his family once leased the place."

"When it was a cobbler's shop?"

"Yes. Magna was with me, and we both felt the timing of the visit to be rather interesting. I imagine he got word that your wife had rented his old family shop and was curious. Magna suggested she look into the man, and I agreed."

Basil shifted his weight, his eyes relaying a fight between disgruntlement and curiosity. "I'm assuming she discovered something of import?"

"Yes," Ginger said. "Colin Venables' brother is Richard Venables, the owner of the Regency Eatery."

"The fellow in the wheelchair?" Basil asked with surprise. "He's the witness to Jimmy Willis's murder!"

Ginger clicked her tongue. "Is that so?"

Basil's gaze landed on Magna, who'd been watching their exchange. His hazel eyes brightened with appreciation. "Good work, Miss Jones. Might I ask how you came upon this information?"

Magna considered Basil coyly. "I have my sources, Chief Inspector."

"But here's the most important part, Basil," Ginger said. "We assumed Richard Venables was in a wheelchair due to injuries from the war, but it was Sid Lester who put him there."

Basil stared at Magna again. "Your sources?"

Magna hesitated before answering. "I have several."

Ginger's gaze lingered on her assistant. Was Magna still working for the secret services? Was that why she'd moved to London? Was her employ at Lady Gold Investigations simply a place for her to work while she waits to receive instructions from those in seniority over her?

Whatever Magna's story, Ginger doubted the woman would confide in her. Ginger understood that information in that arena was given on a need-to-know basis. So long as Magna was useful to Ginger, she couldn't complain about these recent developments.

"If that's true," Basil started, "then Colin Venables jumps to prime suspect. He acted out of revenge for his brother." He snapped his fingers, getting the attention of one of the officers still at the scene. "Constable. Contact the Yard and tell them I want someone to find Mr. Colin Venables and bring him in for questioning."

"Yes, sir." The officer jumped to attention and jogged away.

The ambulance arrived and prepared to take the body to the mortuary.

"If you've finished with me," Dr. Gupta said, "I'll head back to the hospital."

"Righto," Basil replied. "I'll contact you if we need more information."

"Perhaps a visit with Mr. Richard Venables is in order," Ginger said.

Basil still looked unhappy with Ginger, but at least he'd stopped scowling. "My thoughts exactly. Shall we?"

"What about me?" Magna said. "Have I finished here?"

"Yes," Ginger said. "Thank you."

Magna turned on her heel and disappeared through the doorway without another word.

"Charming lady," Basil said with a wry grin.

"She's been through a lot," Ginger said sympathetically, then with more enthusiasm, added, "What's the best way to the Regency Eatery?"

## 25

Though Basil had been to the Regency Eatery when he'd interviewed Colin Venables, it was the first time Ginger had set foot on the premises. Narrow and long, a row of round stools was built in along a long counter—the kitchen area behind it—with tables situated along the opposite wall. A few tables filled out the back. It was busy with customers eager for a hearty breakfast.

When the waiter approached to tell them to be seated, Basil produced his police identification card and nodded towards Richard Venables, who, seated in his wheelchair, was situated alone at a table at the back of the room. "I'd like to speak to Mr. Venables."

"Please wait here," the waiter said, then approached his boss.

"They look a lot alike, now that I'm paying attention," Basil said out of the corner of his mouth.

Ginger agreed. From a distance, Ginger would've thought it was Colin Venables sitting in the chair.

After a few words, the waiter waved them over. Ginger and Basil accepted two of the three empty chairs.

"I'm Chief Inspector Reed of Scotland Yard," Basil started, "and this is Lady Gold of Lady Gold Investigations. She consults with the Metropolitan Police on occasion."

"Pleased to meet you, Lady Gold," Richard Venables said without looking her in the eye.

He adjusted his wheelchair to make room. The apparatus had a wooden base with wicker weaving on the seat and back. It didn't look very comfortable to Ginger, especially if one had to remain in it all day.

Mr. Venables turned to Basil. "I've already talked to one of your constables."

"I do thank you for that," Basil said, "but I hope you don't mind if we ask a few questions too."

"If necessary," Mr. Venables said. "Would you like something to eat or drink?"

Basil shook his head. "No thank you. We don't plan to stay long."

Mr. Venables shifted in his chair awkwardly. "These blasted contraptions. You'd think, in these modern times, they could invent somethin' more comfortable and transportable. I depend on someone to push me around, and it's dashed inconvenient."

"The war?" Ginger asked. Magna had informed

them otherwise, but she wanted to hear Richard Venables answer for himself.

"No, madam, though that's what most people assume." Mr. Venables stared at Ginger. "The truth is, I had an unfortunate encounter with a strong man."

Basil raised a brow. "A strong man?"

"Sadly, it was Sid Lester," Mr. Venables answered. "Long before he got famous in the ring. You see, durin' the war, I developed an attachment to cocaine. It was everywhere in France, and we soldiers were given it in the toughest of times to keep us energised and ready to fight. By the time we returned to England, the blasted government had made it illegal."

"It's a common tale," Ginger said sympathetically.

"Indeed," Richard Venables agreed darkly. "My brother was also a slave to the powder."

"Colin Venables?" Ginger asked.

"Yes, Colin," Mr. Venables said. "We were three brothers, but our oldest came back from the war in a box."

"My deepest condolences," Ginger said with sincerity. Her first husband had come home in a box as well.

"Why did Sid Lester come after you?" Basil asked.

"He worked as a debt collector," Mr. Venables explained. His open expression collapsed into a scowl. "But it wasn't me who owed him money."

Ginger raised a brow. "Oh?"

"It was Colin. He owed money and couldn't pay it back."

"For cocaine?" Ginger clarified.

"Yes, madam," Mr. Venables returned. "I managed to kick the habit." Scowling, he added, "It was harder for my brother."

Perhaps Colin Venables' love for boxing wasn't the only thing that kept him working in the ring. Perhaps it also facilitated his addiction.

"If your brother was the addict, why did Mr. Lester attack you?" Ginger asked.

"Because he was an addict too," Richard Venables said, his eyes flashing. "He got us mixed up. Went after me instead of Colin!"

"Do you know who Lester worked for?" Basil asked.

Mr. Venables frowned. "Someone called The Griffin. I never met the man myself."

"Did your brother hold Mr. Lester responsible for your current situation?" Ginger asked.

For a brief second, Richard Venables sneered. "I don't think so. He ended up workin' for the fellow."

"What did you see in the park this morning, Mr. Venables?" Basil asked.

"I was sittin' outside in the back garden of my flat . . ." He motioned to the back of the restaurant. ". . . drinkin' tea. I like to start my days quiet-like, but a man came runnin' through that old door out of the blue. The squeakin' got my attention, and then bam, a gunshot. The chap fell and didn't get up. I called for Davy—he's my assistant, and he also helps in the kitchen—just to ensure I wasn't hearin' or seein' things. I was shocked when I heard it was Lester's trainer, Jimmy Willis."

"Did you recognise the gunman?" Ginger asked. "Was his silhouette at all familiar?"

Mr. Venables frowned. "No, madam."

Ginger sat up at the sight of Constable Braxton entering the restaurant. She nudged Basil's arm, drawing his attention.

"Excuse me," Basil said, getting to his feet.

Ginger watched as Braxton whispered something in her husband's ear. Basil whispered back, then Braxton left. Basil returned to the table, holding out his hand. "It seems we need to leave, Lady Gold."

Ginger accepted Basil's chivalry, then turned to Mr. Venables. "Thank you for your time. Are you feeling any better?" Her question was loaded with meaning.

Mr. Venables seemed to understand. "The only thing I take now, madam, is aspirin."

"So good to hear," Ginger said. She reached out her hand, and Richard Venables accepted.

Ginger was eager to hear what Constable Braxton had had to say that caused their sudden departure. Basil finally eased her curiosity when they stepped outside.

"It's Kenmore," Basil said. "He wants to confess."

MURDER AT THE BOXING CLUB

. . .

BASIL SAT with Ginger at the metal table in the interrogation room. Ginger was in her role as a police consultant, while Braxton looked on from his position by the door. On the other side of the table sat two men: Billy Kenmore and a man dressed in an expensive-looking suit, carrying an expensive-looking leather briefcase.

"Good day, my name is Peter Falconer," the slick man said. Middle-aged, with wire-framed spectacles and oiled-back black hair, his expression was one of seriousness and curtness. All business. "Mr. Kenmore has hired me for legal counsel in this matter."

Basil had heard of Peter Falconer before. The solicitor had defended several dubious characters over the years and had a reputation of pulling rabbits out of hats. If you could afford Peter Falconer to defend you, you were far more likely to get a lighter sentence than expected, if not complete exoneration. He was the kind of solicitor that a policeman like Basil abhorred.

"Of course, I know who you are, Chief Inspector," Falconer said with a sly smile. "But I don't believe I've had the pleasure . . ." Falconer extended his hand towards Ginger.

Ginger politely nodded as she shook his hand. "I'm pleased to meet you as well."

Basil caught Kenmore's eye. "The Griffin ensured you got the best representation possible, eh?"

Kenmore shook his head. "Actually, no. I called 'im meself. I'm parting ways with Sharp."

Basil raised a brow. "Is that so?" Mortimer Sharp wouldn't take kindly to that, and Kenmore would know it.

"Not that any of it matters," Falconer interjected. "The main point here is you're holding my client for a crime that he most certainly did not commit, and that needs to end now."

"That's a bit optimistic," Ginger said.

"Nonetheless, after you hear what my client has to say, I think certain important details may crystallise in your investigation, and . . ." He looked at Kenmore, then leaned forward in his chair with his hands folded on the table. "You will be compelled to drop murder charges against my client."

"I dinn't shoot Lester," Kenmore claimed again.

"We have a witness who saw you leaving the alley in your car at full speed during the time the shooting took place," Basil said. "We have proof that the motorcar belongs to you."

Kenmore shared another look with his solicitor, who nodded for him to go ahead.

"It was me motorcar, all right," Kenmore admitted. "But it wasn't me drivin'. I came out of the club to find me motorcar gone. Someone stole it. I found it later parked near Mile End Station."

"Are you saying Mortimer Sharp did not instruct you to kill Sid Lester?" Ginger asked.

"No, I'm not saying that," Kenmore said. "That's what I'm trying to get at. 'E did tell me to knock off Lester; only someone beat me to it."

Basil and Ginger exchanged a look, then Basil said. "You're saying you intended to kill Lester, but before you could, someone else stole your motorcar just as Lester was leaving the boxing club and shot him as he raced away?"

Kenmore nodded. "That's what I'm saying."

"And you were just hanging around the exhibition match whilst this was going on?" Ginger asked. "You must've seen Mr. Lester leave the premises if your task was to 'knock him off'."

"I got a little caught up in the fight, see?" Kenmore pointed to his temple. "I saw Lester leavin' from the corner of me eye, and I started runnin' for the door—I planned to run to my motorcar and follow 'im—'e didn't drive, you see, but then I 'eard a bunch of blasted gunshots! I peeked out the window and saw Lester on the ground. Well, there was no way I was going to go through that door now, was I?"

Basil found the story rather unbelievable. "And Sharp?"

"I dinn't tell 'im. I found my motorcar a short time later, the gun tucked under the seat as always, and decided to just let things lie where they were."

"You let Mortimer Sharp believe you'd completed the task," Ginger said, "and accepted payment?"

"I suppose it wasn't very 'onourable for me to take

payment for a job someone else did." Kenmore shrugged a shoulder.

"No honour amongst thieves," Basil said, considering the henchman. Kenmore had taken an enormous personal risk exposing The Griffin, and recent details about Colin Venables made his story more plausible. "Why confess to this now?" he asked.

Falconer interjected. "My client has information about Mortimer Sharp that you will undoubtedly find useful. Enough to justify an arrest."

"For what? Attempted murder?" Basil said. "That's hard to prove in court just based on your client's testimony."

"Do I have your word that you will speak to your superiors about my client's cooperation?" Falconer asked. "Mr. Kenmore will need police protection until Sharp is in jail."

"One can't put a person in prison for having an unexecuted bad intention," Basil said. "It has to be something true and provable, but yes . . ." He leaned back and eyed the men across the table. "I give you my word."

"Mortimer Sharp was the one who shot Marvin Elliott, and what's more . . ." Kenmore burst out suddenly. "What's more, 'e plans to finish the job as soon as 'e gets a chance."

Ginger's green eyes darted to Basil, flashing with alarm. "How do you know that?" she asked.

"Sharp was furious that 'e didn't complete the job

the first time," Kenmore said. "'E told me before I got arrested that 'e was going to finish it."

"Why didn't he get you to do it?" Basil asked. "To target Marvin Elliot?"

"'E said this one was personal," Kenmore said. "I dinn't ask 'im why."

Basil leaned in. "What kind of pistol does Sharp like to use?"

"'E has one of them German makes. 'E boasted that 'e could plug a 'alf crown from ten paces." Kenmore scratched his chin. "An odd-lookin' gun with a metric calibre. It was what the Boche used in the war."

"Do you mean a Parabellum?" Ginger asked.

Basil cast his wife a side glance. Her familiarity with weapons and all things related to the Great War was something he'd learned to stop questioning.

"Yeah, that's it," Kenmore said. "It 'ad the word *Luger* stamped on it."

## 26

Mortimer Sharp.

The name produced terror in the hearts of men who knew better, and the wise wouldn't even speak it aloud—calling him The Griffin, a mythical creature formed from a lion and an eagle. Strength and power. The image pleased him.

Fearless, he made the weak shake at the knees, and in Mortimer's best moments, they pleaded and cried like babies before he, like a god on earth, snuffed their lives at will.

Dressed in a white lab coat with a stethoscope hanging from his neck, spectacles on his face, and a clipboard in his hand, Mortimer stepped inside the Royal Free Hospital on Gray's Inn Road. The costume had been nicked at his command by the halfwit Fletcher, one of many coppers Mortimer had in his pocket.

It was his secret thrill to deceive people with disguise and guile. Even though he was a tall man, he could make himself look a little shorter if he stooped his shoulders and hobbled slowly. A cane was a nice touch. Along with a grey wig, a fake moustache, and tramp's clothing, he'd easily entered Marvin Elliot's residential building, his Luger in the waistband of his trousers.

His ability to deceive and manipulate was a gift of his nature. He lacked sympathy and empathy, also a gift. His only regret was that, like many great historic artists, few people would ever appreciate his brilliance until after he was gone. His successful tactics at bamboozling police would be studied in their training schools, much like Jack the Ripper's activities were being examined now.

Of course, The Griffin was an elegant master compared to the barbaric Jack.

Heading up the stairwell to the top floor, Mortimer was annoyed by a plump nurse who entered at the second level.

"Good evening, Doctor," the nurse said with a warm smile as she briskly kept step with him. "You're on the late shift, I see."

He smiled back with feigned kindness. "I have a few patients I want to check up on tonight before I head home."

"Honestly, most doctors are underappreciated for the care and the hours they put in." The nurse giggled as if her blatant attempt at flattery could tempt him.

"The same goes for you nurses," he returned. He nearly exited on the next floor to escape the silly woman, or better yet, he could end his misery with a quick twist of her slender neck.

Luckily for her, the nurse stepped out instead, not knowing how close she'd come to meeting her maker. "Good evening, Doctor," she said.

Mortimer merely nodded, turning the corner of the staircase and continuing upwards.

He felt no compunction for what he was about to do; there was no hesitancy in his step as he exited the stairwell and headed directly towards the room where the young braggart was being held. Elliot deserved to die for two . . . no . . . three reasons.

First, he talked far too much and far too loudly for someone who knew the inner workings of the covert drug business conducted at the Bethnal Green Boxing Club. Second, he might have been a gifted fighter, but he was also a fool for refusing to allow himself to be managed by The Griffin. If there was one thing that Mortimer Sharp could not abide, it was a fool. Third, and this reason was supreme, he was related by his adoptive family to Chief Inspector Basil Reed and his arrogant wife, Lady Gold. It made him an easy target to begin the vengeance Mortimer had in store for the man who had put him in prison.

As he walked down the corridor, spectacles on his

face, keeping his gaze on the clipboard, Mortimer's doctor disguise worked brilliantly. No one paid him any attention—neither the night nurses, orderlies, nor the old caretaker.

Fletcher sat on a wooden chair in front of Elliot's door, and Mortimer suppressed the urge to smirk as the man's expression turned to that of a frightened mouse when he saw Mortimer approaching. Rising, he said, "sir?"

"Stay seated, you fool," Mortimer growled in a low voice.

Fletcher dropped onto the chair. "Erm . . . of course, sir."

Mortimer slid his hand into the large side pocket of his lab coat and felt the reassuringly cool walnut grip of the Luger.

Fletcher had been instructed to put sleeping powder in Elliot's tea—Mortimer was in no mood for resistance, and it was vital not to have a screaming target blow his cover. The dolt was also told to ensure the door hinges were oiled so Mortimer could slip into the private room without a sound. The darkness was nearly complete except for the muted light coming through the curtain from the new electric streetlights on Gray's Inn Road.

Mortimer approached the bed and regarded the still form under the blankets, facing the window. His wisps of hair poked out from the bandages on his head.

An easy target.

Carefully, Mortimer removed the Luger and the suppressor from his pockets. It only took a moment to screw the device onto the barrel.

"You're a scrapper, Elliot," he said to the unconscious form on the bed. "And I admire that—a real fighter. I've killed plenty of men or had them killed. Sinclair, Albright, and Willis. You're the only one who didn't die when you were supposed to. Got a horseshoe in the backside, eh? Well, your luck's about to run out."

## 27

Ignoring the thundering of his heart beating in his chest, Basil stepped out from behind the hospital curtain. "Stop right there!"

His voice sounded sharp to his own ears, ringing out like a thunderclap in the darkness. Holding his service revolver firmly with both hands, he commanded, "Drop your weapon!"

The Griffin froze, his hawkish eyes darting to the side of the room where Basil stood but not flinching as he held the Luger at the form in the bed.

In all his years as a policeman, Basil had never seen an expression of such ferocity and anger on someone's visage. Mortimer Sharp was a feral creature—unpredictable, wild, and vicious.

"It's over, Sharp," Basil said. "Put down your weapon."

A shiver shot down Basil's spine as the corner of

Sharp's mouth curled upwards in a cruel sneer, releasing an animal-like growl.

From another darkened corner of the room came the sound of a pistol hammer clicking back.

"I would listen to him if I were you." Ginger's voice was even and calm. It wasn't the first time Basil had wondered how and when his wife had developed such nerves of steel.

Sharp didn't move a muscle. Basil kept his finger slightly pressured against his trigger. If Sharp turned his weapon on Ginger, Basil would drop him on the spot without hesitation.

"You think you've won, eh?" Sharp said. An evil grin crossed his face, and his eyes flashed with determination. He snorted. "In the end, I always win, Reed. You should know that by now."

The Luger made a *pfft* sound as it kicked slightly upwards.

In an instant, Basil pulled the trigger of his own revolver; the sound of the blast was loud, like a barking dog.

Sharp's right shoulder jerked violently backwards as his Luger fell to the floor. He stood for one long moment, his eyes remaining fierce and savage before they finally rolled back in his head as he collapsed.

. . .

Braxton rolled out from under the hospital bed, his uniform dusty and wrinkled, and stared at Ginger with wide eyes. "Are you all right, madam?"

Ginger nodded. "I am." Keeping her gun poised, Ginger approached the man on the floor. Mortimer Sharp looked incapacitated, but she wouldn't put it past a devious fellow like him to fake injury or death but maintaining enough strength to grab her by the ankle.

"Careful, Ginger." Basil, also with his revolver at the ready, approached The Griffin, still sprawled on the floor, where blood leaked from the bullet wound, creating a red pool on the white vinyl floor.

With Basil's weapon leveled at Sharp's head, Ginger pressed the two fingers of her free hand to check for a pulse.

"It's faint," she said, "but he's alive."

The gunshot had warranted the attention of the nurses and doctors on the ward, and the room was soon crowded.

"Doctor!" Basil's voice rose about the murmurs. "This man needs medical attention." Slipping his revolver into his jacket pocket he then announced to the others, "Please be calm and stay back. I'm Chief Inspector Reed. This man is in my custody, and the circumstances are a matter for the police." To Braxton he said, "Ring the Yard and report."

The hospital staff hadn't been informed of the tricky manoeuvre on Ginger and Basil's part as they couldn't know for sure if any of them had been unduly influenced by Mortimer Sharp and his gang.

Ginger and Basil hung back as the doctor and nurses lifted Mortimer Sharp off the floor and onto the bed which had been occupied by a life-sized stuffed pillow.

The doctor turned to Basil. "We need to remove the bullet. We're wheeling him to surgery now. If we delay, it might cost him his life."

"Do what you must," Basil said.

Mortimer Sharp had a right to life-saving surgery, just as he had a right to a trial. They had enough evidence to convict him of multiple murders now that he had made his confession, which Ginger, Basil and Braxton had overheard.

He was alive but would spend the rest of his days in prison awaiting an appointment with a noose. The surge of relief Ginger felt was so intense, she grabbed her husband's arm to keep from trembling. She and her family would be safe from Basil's long-time nemesis at last.

## 28

As Ginger had promised, she was on the train to Dover by the weekend. Basil would join the family in France in a week's time once he closed the case on Mortimer Sharp.

Finally, her nightmare was over.

Ginger leaned her head back as she gazed out of the train window as the pastoral view meandered by. Soon she'd be reunited with Rosa, Scout, and the rest of her family and would relax in the villa gardens when she and Felicia weren't in the city shopping.

Meanwhile, the train journey gave her time to think about everything that had happened.

Mortimer Sharp hadn't killed Marvin—it had been a down blanket and a dummy made of pillows that lay "wounded" in the hospital. Constable Fletcher had played his part well, cooperating with the police on this operation in exchange for a lighter sentence. The constable had had the extra incentive to do the right thing as Ginger had been watching him, disguised as a nurse herself.

Marvin was safely back home in his flat, with an aide Ginger had hired to care for him. It would be some time before he could manage on his own, and Ginger worried that he might never fully recover.

A carriage attendant pushed a newspaper trolley, and Ginger bought a copy of *The Daily News* and opened to the story—byline Blake Brown—about The Griffin's arrest. Ginger had to admire the journalist. He had a load of determination and bulldog tenacity, and she wasn't surprised he'd landed the scoop.

The case had been complicated and convoluted. It turned out that Richard Venables held a grudge against his brother, blaming him for Lester mistakenly attacking him. Had Colin had the backbone to quit drugs and pay his bills, Richard wouldn't have been in a wheelchair under Colin's thumb for the rest of his life.

Basil had held Colin Venables and questioned him for long enough that the man exhibited unbearable withdrawal symptoms. Finally getting the upper hand, Richard Venables had used this vulnerable moment to convince his brother to confess to killing Sid Lester.

It was a sad tale between two brothers.

Colin Venables confessed he'd been waiting for a chance to get his revenge. When Mr. Lester had threatened to come after him for money Colin owed for his drug use but couldn't pay, Colin took action. It was pure luck of circumstance that he had seen Mr. Kenmore's motorcar parked in the alley. He knew Kenmore kept a weapon hidden under the front seat, and Mr. Venables' plan for retribution was formed. He only had to wait for Mr. Lester to exit the building.

As fate would have it, Billy Kenmore, on Mortimer Sharp's instructions, had also intended to kill Mr. Lester that same day. Instead of coming clean to Mortimer Sharp, Mr. Kenmore took the credit for the killing and accepted payment.

Mortimer Sharp was healing up in a prison hospital. He'd confessed that he'd gone after Marvin mostly because he loathed Basil, admitting to being careless, blindsided by his drive for vengeance. Ginger and Basil were both witnesses to his confession about killing Jimmy Willis. During the interrogation, he finally admitted it—especially once he'd been convinced of the evidence against him—all because the cocky Mr. Willis claimed he had witnessed Mr. Kenmore driving the getaway car and wanted Mr. Sharp to pay him to keep quiet. Mr. Willis had lied about something that Mr. Sharp had believed to be true, getting himself killed. The man had paid dearly for his deception and greed.

Mr. Kenmore had been released, feeling his life was safer now that Mortimer Sharp was going down for murder. He'd been tasked by Sharp to kill Sid Lester, Sharp believing the boxer had thrown the fight and cost him a good deal of money on lost bets. He'd been correct on that matter, as Dr. Gupta had later confirmed that, though Mr. Lester had plenty of injuries, new and old, the shoulder in question had been uninjured. With Mr. Lester dead, they'd never learn of his reasonings. Had he thrown the fight to avoid an embarrassing loss to a younger, faster fighter? Or had he been involved in a rigging scheme with hopes of getting paid under the table by some unknown sponsor?

Though it had been Mr. Kenmore's intention to kill Mr. Lester on Mortimer Sharp's orders, he wasn't the one who actually committed the crime, so there was nothing the police could do but let the man go. Not that he was innocent of crime. Ginger was sure there were other unsolved cases with Kenmore attached to them, but all the police could do for now was to keep watch.

With Sharp and his gang brought low, Ginger hoped the drug business would subside. It would be naive to believe it would go away for good—there were many men like Richard Venables who had come back from the war addicted to cocaine and weren't able to kick the habit. And in a world where money was made by sports betting, there would always be those cheating their way to a win.

Thomas Friar had managed to cover his tracks and Basil was unable to put together a case of drug dealing against him. Poor Marvin was amongst his victims, but it didn't appear that he'd ever be of sound enough mind to testify in a court of law. Sadly, there would always be men like Mr. Friar in the world, exploiting people for his own gain.

The train reached Dover Ferry Terminal. Presenting her ticket, Ginger walked on board the vessel heading to France. She wore a peacock-blue chemise frock with a blue-and-white-striped sailor collar, which was both fashionable and suitable for such a journey.

The weather was pleasant enough to spend most of the time on deck; the view became water and sky only as the white cliffs of Dover gradually disappeared. She enjoyed a small lunch of a salmon paste sandwich and a delightful cup of tea and spent the rest of her time flipping through the most recent *Life* magazine. By the time she reached the French shores, Ginger was feeling relaxed and quite ready for a holiday. She and Felicia were sure to have a splendid time shopping in the divine Parisian dress shops!

After one final train trip through the lovely pastoral French countryside, the iconic Eiffel Tower finally came into view.

Ginger had plenty of memories of the City of Love, none of them involving love, however. She'd been there during the dark war years, of course, and then more recently on shopping sprees for new fashions and fabrics to display and sell at Feathers & Flair. How nice to finally come when pistols weren't firing, and when business wasn't at the forefront. And with Basil arriving soon, she might experience love in the city after all!

She'd sent a telegram letting Charles and Felicia know the time of her arrival, and Ginger scoured the crowd, looking for their familiar faces. Had her telegram reached the Davenport-Witts?

The station was crowded with French people. Their particular patriotic stare, their pride of culture, and their flair for language filled the area. Ginger warmed to the melodic sounds of the French language, delighted with herself that she understood everything she overheard, and that time and lack of use hadn't caused her skills to noticeably subside.

She was about to search for another taxicab to make the final leg of the journey on her own, when she heard a robust American voice break through the French conversations around her.

"Ginger Gold! Is that you?"

Ginger pivoted towards the American accent. Standing before her was a tall lady with curly dark hair and a wide smile. Unlike her French counterparts who were colorfully dressed and in flowing frocks, the American wore a brown blazer and trousers!

"Haley Higgins!" Ginger shrieked. "You are a sight for sore eyes!"

Forgoing the double-cheek kiss, the two friends warmly embraced as Americans do.

Ginger pulled back and stared up at her tall friend. "Haley. It's so wonderful to see you again."

"You look as beautiful as always!" Haley returned. "And I hear that you and your lovely husband have been busy. You've just caught a multi-murderer! It's in all the papers."

Ginger laughed. How small the world was getting. News travelled to the Continent so quickly these days. "Indeed," she said. "We are due for a holiday and I'm so delighted that you're continuing your studies in Europe. I couldn't be more pleased."

Haley linked her arm through Ginger's as she guided her to the station's exit. "Nor I," she said. "I can't wait to catch up."

"Have you enjoyed your time in Paris so far?" Ginger asked as they stepped outside. Then with a sly grin added, "Are you keeping out of trouble?"

Haley laughed, her dark curls in her faux bob getting caught up in the wind. "I certainly have been, and it's been dang boring." She flashed a knowing smile. "But now that you're here, I'm sure that won't last long."

The End

If you enjoyed reading *Murder at the Boxing Club* please help others enjoy it too.

**Recommend it:** Help others find the book by recommending it to friends, readers' groups, discussion boards and by **suggesting it to your local library.**

**Review it:** Please tell other readers why you liked this book by reviewing **at leestraussbooks.com**

*No spoilers, please.

Don't miss the next Ginger Gold mystery~
MURDER IN FRANCE

**Murder is so *sang-froid*!**

When the Reed family—temporarily exiled to France—was once again safe, Ginger decides to turn the event into a much needed holiday. And the absolute cake was Ginger's reunion with her American friend Haley Higgins, who is working in France on a practicum to become a lady doctor.

Ginger celebrates the happy reunion by throwing a party at their villa in Paris, but the joyous activities are halted when a body is discovered. Like old times, Ginger puts her detective skills to work while Haley provides her forensic knowledge. As party guests continue to become more suspicious and worthy suspects, Ginger's own past is soon on trial.

Has a long-ago, war-time "error" resurfaced to steal more than Ginger's *joie de vivre*?

**Shop at leestraussbooks.com**

---

Don't miss the FINAL ROSA REED MYSTERY!

MURDER AT THE WEDDINGS

## Seeing Double is Murder!

If one wedding is good, a double wedding is better! Rosa and Miguel agree that walking down the aisle with Bill and Carlotta solves a lot of social and familial problems, but the drama is notched up when a dead body arrives with dessert!

Don't miss this final installment of a Rosa Reed Mystery series where Rosa finally gets her happily ever after.

**Shop at leestraussbooks.com**

MORE FROM LEE STRAUSS

**Shop at leestraussbooks.com**

**GINGER GOLD MYSTERY SERIES (cozy 1920s historical)**

*Cozy. Charming. Filled with Bright Young Things. This Jazz Age murder mystery will entertain and delight you with its 1920s flair and pizzazz!*

Murder on the SS Rosa

Murder at Hartigan House

Murder at Bray Manor

Murder at Feathers & Flair

Murder at the Mortuary

Murder at Kensington Gardens

Murder at St. George's Church

The Wedding of Ginger & Basil

Murder Aboard the Flying Scotsman

Murder at the Boat Club

Murder on Eaton Square

Murder by Plum Pudding

Murder on Fleet Street

Murder at Brighton Beach

Murder in Hyde Park

Murder at the Royal Albert Hall

Murder in Belgravia

Murder on Mallowan Court

Murder at the Savoy

Murder at the Circus

Murder in France

Murder at Yuletide

Murder at Madame Tussauds

Murder at St. Paul's Cathedral

## LADY GOLD INVESTIGATES (Ginger Gold companion short stories)

Volume 1

Volume 2

Volume 3

Volume 4

Volume 5

## HIGGINS & HAWKE MYSTERY SERIES (cozy 1930s historical)

*The 1930s meets Rizzoli & Isles in this friendship depression era cozy mystery series.*

Death at the Tavern

Death on the Tower

Death on Hanover

Death by Dancing

Death on Tremont Row

THE ROSA REED MYSTERIES

(1950s cozy historical)

Murder at High Tide

Murder on the Boardwalk

Murder at the Bomb Shelter

Murder on Location

Murder and Rock 'n Roll

Murder at the Races

Murder at the Dude Ranch

Murder in London

Murder at the Fiesta

Murder at the Weddings

**A NURSERY RHYME MYSTERY SERIES (mystery/sci fi)**

*Marlow finds himself teamed up with intelligent and savvy Sage Farrell, a girl so far out of his league he feels blinded in her presence - literally - damned glasses! Together they work to find the identity of @gingerbreadman. Can they stop the killer before he strikes again?*

Gingerbread Man

Life Is but a Dream

Hickory Dickory Dock

Twinkle Little Star

## LIGHT & LOVE (sweet romance)

*Set in the dazzling charm of Europe, follow Katja, Gabriella, Eva, Anna and Belle as they find strength, hope and love.*

Love Song

Your Love is Sweet

In Light of Us

Lying in Starlight

## PLAYING WITH MATCHES (WW2 history/romance)

*A sobering but hopeful journey about how one young German boy copes with the war and propaganda. Based on true events.*

A Piece of Blue String (companion short story)

THE CLOCKWISE COLLECTION (YA time travel

romance)

*Casey Donovan has issues: hair, height and uncontrollable trips to the 19th century! And now this ~ she's accidentally taken Nate Mackenzie, the cutest boy in the school, back in time. Awkward.*

Clockwise

Clockwiser

Like Clockwork

Counter Clockwise

Clockwork Crazy

Clocked (companion novella)

<u>Standalones</u>

Seaweed

Love, Tink

## ABOUT THE AUTHOR

Lee Strauss is a USA TODAY bestselling author of The Ginger Gold Mysteries series, The Higgins & Hawke Mystery series, The Rosa Reed Mystery series (cozy historical mysteries), A Nursery Rhyme Mystery series (mystery suspense), The Perception series (young adult dystopian), The Light & Love series (sweet romance), The Clockwise Collection (YA time travel romance), and young adult historical fiction with over a million books read. She has translated titles and a growing audio library.

When Lee's not writing or reading she likes to cycle, hike, and stare at the ocean. She loves to drink caffè lattes and red wines in exotic places, and eat dark chocolate anywhere.

For more info on books by Lee Strauss and her social media links, visit leestraussbooks.com. To make sure you don't miss the next new release, be sure to sign up for her newsletter!

Did you know you can follow your favourite authors on Bookbub? If you subscribe to Bookbub — (and if you don't, why don't you? - They'll send you daily emails alerting you to sales and new releases on just the kind of books you like to read!) — follow me to make sure you don't miss the next Ginger Gold Mystery!

www.leestraussbooks.com
leestraussbooks@gmail.com
facebook.com/AuthorLeeStrauss

Printed in the USA
CPSIA information can be obtained
at www.ICGtesting.com
LVHW041748030324
773431LV00003B/457

9 781774 094082